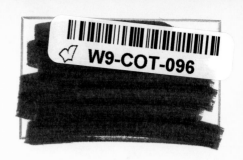

MENNONITE
MARTHA

❀

Also by Margaret Pitcairn Strachan

CLASS PRESIDENT

MENNONITE

MARTHA

By Margaret Pitcairn Strachan

Illustrated by Charles Geer

IVES WASHBURN, INC.

New York

For my mother,
and with thanks to
Grace and Gracious,
Ruby and Roy

CONTENTS
❁

MENNONITE
MARTHA
❀

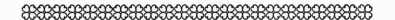

1. A FAMILY PLAN

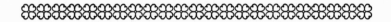

MARTHA was feeding the pigs in the Sherfey's big red barn that Saturday morning when she heard Grandpa Sherfey pull into the driveway in his buggy. Because she was twelve, the pigs were Martha's sole responsibility. But now she quickly threw the rest of the feed into the trough, dropped the bucket, and ran to the window.

A brisk March breeze blew over the Bucks County Hills in Pennsylvania, so that Grandpa had put the side curtains up on his falling-top carriage. Grandpa's carriage was the latest style for 1884 despite the fact that he wore the "plain" Mennonite garb of a coat without a collar buttoned up to his neck. Martha thought he always looked pleased with himself when he drove his fast-stepping mare and falling-top carriage.

With a shiver of excitement Martha cautiously opened the window a crack so that she could hear Grandpa and Father talking out in the yard. For that morning at breakfast Father had said he intended to tell Grandpa he planned to buy one of the new all-metal reapers advertised in the farm papers.

3

"I-yi-yi-yi," Mother had whispered, her eyes wide with fright, "what will he say yet?"

"I have my own place now," Father answered, "and can do things my way. Those thirteen years we lived with Grandpa Sherfey I farmed his way."

"But Grandpa has a reaper," Martha said.

"*Ja*," Father nodded, "but he bought it secondhand years ago and it only cuts the grain. He thinks a man's labor tying grain is cheaper than buying a reaper with the binder attachment. His reaper hasn't even a self-raker and it takes hours longer to harvest every acre."

"How much is the new McCormick reaper?" Mother asked.

Martha knew it had taken all the family money to purchase the farm, the cows, Goldie the sow, the two horses, a hundred hens, and the most necessary furnishings for the house. In order to make enough for them to live on until the farm produced, Father taught the one-room school she and Johnny, her ten-year-old brother, attended.

"Martha," Father said, "bring me the paper. I'll show you an advertisement. If we buy the reaper it means all of us must work together to pay for it."

When Father spread the paper on the table in front of Mother's place, Martha and Johnny moved closer to look over her shoulder. A full-page advertisement described the wonders of the new piece of machinery. A picture at the top showed a pair of sleek horses trotting with a reaper. A boy about Johnny's size rode on the

back of one horse and cracked a whip in fine style. A waistcoated gentleman in a top hat leaned forward gracefully in the seat to look proudly at the field spread out around him covered with neatly tied bundles of grain lying in straight rows.

"Show me! Show me!" four-year-old Debbie demanded from her place beside Father, and in his high chair six-month-old Peter clapped his hands as though he knew just what they were discussing.

"It says this is the strongest reaper ever made," Martha pointed out, "and a child could reap and bind a field of wheat."

Staring at the picture, Martha thought that boys had all the fun. Although Johnny was younger, he would ride the horse while she sat inside sewing a shirt for him or a dress for herself. And a gray or brown dress at that!

"*Ach*, but it costs a hundred and twenty-five dollars!" Mother suddenly gasped. "So much money we could not get!"

"Things cost such a much these days," Father agreed, "but you see this would be an investment. I could hire out this summer and cut grain for others. Next winter I'm sure the school board will hire a woman to save money and I'll be out of a job."

Mother looked at the picture again and read the words beneath it. She looked very troubled.

"Do you want my egg money?" she asked at last.

Martha caught her breath. Mother's egg money was

put aside to furnish the parlor. At present there was not so much as a chair in that room.

"Would you give up buying parlor furniture for a reaper?" Father asked in a low voice as he shook his head. "Such a sacrifice of you I would not ask. Never have you had your own parlor."

"A sacrifice it would not be." Mother smiled. "I know I'll get it later. The farm must come first."

"The egg money would help," Father admitted. "But we would need a lot more than that."

"It takes a lot of eggs at ten cents a dozen to make a dollar," said Mother.

For a moment Martha expected Father to make her figure how many; arithmetic was the one subject she hated. So since she had an idea about her own contribution, she spoke quickly.

"When the strawberries ripen you can have the money from my berries. Even the new plants I put in may do well," she said.

But her heart gave a great lurch. Secretly she had planned on spending the money for gay pink material for a dress. Never in her whole life had she owned a dress that was not brown or gray.

"When Bessie drops her calf next month," Johnny said, "I'll raise it for you and sell it for veal in the fall. Would that help?"

Bessie's calf was promised to Johnny, and Martha knew he would like to buy a fishing rod. But Mennonites did not fish or hunt and so they never owned rods or guns. Martha realized that Johnny only gave his wish a passing thought. He accepted the fact that he could not have such things.

Why can't I be like that, she thought, instead of wanting to be like Freda Landis in a pretty dress, wearing a gold ring with a red stone in it! I wish I were born a Baptist like Freda. *Ach*, we're cousins yet, but so different!

"Those are good ideas," Father said. "If we all work together, we'll earn that reaper. I'm going to ask Grandpa Sherfey if he will loan me the money to get it. I'd pay him the same interest he receives for his money at the bank."

"Never will he help you buy such newfangled machinery," said Mother. "Something else maybe, but not that."

"Likely not, but it won't hurt to ask once. Nothing ventured, nothing gained."

And so now Martha listened, her heart beating rapidly. Never until six months ago had Father ever done anything Grandpa Sherfey did not approve of. Then he managed to buy this farm. It was the Mennonite custom for sons to live with their fathers long after marriage, working for little or no pay, and Grandpa had been angry when they left.

Surely when he heard Father's new plan he would be angrier than ever. How could Father risk his fury? Would calling it an investment help?

But Grandpa did not give Father a chance to explain

about the business investment. He exploded at once. He jumped down from the carriage and the two stood close to the barn.

"Such blamed foolishness!" he shouted. "You want I should lend you one hundred and twenty-five dollars that I saved by doing my own work by hand? Well, I guess anyhow not!"

"Interest I would pay you," Father pointed out. "You would not lose by it."

"For an all-metal reaper or whatever I won't loan a cent!" Grandpa waved his arms in the air to show his disgust. "Nor will the bank take a note from you. Just starting out on this place, you are, and who is to know that you will make a go of things? You should have stayed working for me. Money is tight these days and you should learn to get along without such folderols. I myself can bind as good as any machine ever invented."

"But with a binder on the reaper two men can harvest twelve to fourteen acres of grain in a day," Father protested. "Your fields I could do also."

"*Nein!*" Grandpa ended the conversation by turning his back on Father and climbing into his carriage. Without so much as a backward glance he slapped the reins smartly and drove off.

Martha watched her father standing quietly, deep in thought. What would he do now? Give up? Suddenly he straightened his shoulders and headed for the chicken house to give Johnny a hand. His head was up and he swung his arms easily.

No, Father's not going to give up! He's like Grandpa in that for all! Once they make up their mind to something, nothing will change them.

At noon dinner Martha found her guess was correct. Father said he was not discouraged. He would pray about it and God would help him find a way to manage.

"Joe Landis has a McCormick reaper," Father said. "When I saw it, I realized it might be the answer to the problem of how to support us without me teaching."

It surprised Martha that Father wanted something that Freda's father had as much as she herself wanted what Freda had! It was discouraging to consider the fact that when you grew up you still wanted many things and were unable to get them. But her own desires seemed selfish when she compared them with Father's. If he succeeded in buying a reaper, it would benefit the entire family. But if she used her strawberry money to buy a pretty calico print, or four yards of gay pink lawn or challis, who would benefit?

What kind of machine could do all the work Father described? She opened the paper again to the advertisement and studied the picture to try to understand how the reaper and binder worked.

"Will Maud and May be able to pull it, you think?" she asked.

"Both together, yes," Father said, and Martha laughed.

Maud and May, the two mares Father had bought from Joe Godshalk on the next farm, never would do anything separately. They had to do things together, or they balked and stood still. When Johnny took Maud to the watering trough the first night they had the horses, she refused to drink. Then he tried to make May drink, and she tossed her head and pulled back. Then Martha led Maud out again while May was standing there, and both horses took long swallows, blowing the water out through their noses in a sort of snort when they finished.

That was the way it had been ever since. If Johnny put oats in a feed bag and slipped it over Maud's head, she did not take so much as a smidgeon until May had her own feed bag. And when Father tried to drive one of the mares alone, she refused to move until he cracked the whip over her head with a loud snap. Then she ran around the barnyard and shied away from the gate. In the end Father hitched up the second mare and they both stepped out as smartly as you please.

"*Ach*, someday could I stop by Freda's to see the reaper?" Martha asked.

"*Ja*," Father said, and his eyes twinkled, "do that and see if you want to contribute your earnings to buy such a piece of blamed foolishness!"

"I-yi-yi-yi," Mother spoke hastily, "Grandpa means well. He is just old-fashioned for all. Remember, Martha, it isn't long after school till dark. You must be home in time to feed Goldie and her pigs!"

Martha promised promptly. Only once before had she ever been in the Landis house. When Freda's father married out of the Mennonite Church he was cut off from his relatives.

Martha suddenly had a twinge of conscience, feeling that she was being unfair to her best friend, Sarah Mayer. But she felt certain that Sarah would go to Freda's if she had such an opportunity. And Martha would tell her all about it afterward.

"See here," Father said, "do you think I'll have to wear a top hat to drive Maud and May with that reaper?"

Johnny hooted and Martha giggled. Even Mother laughed at the picture of Father in his Mennonite coat without any buttons, wearing a fashionable top hat.

"*Ach*," said Mother, "there'll be no money for so much as a new bonnet for Martha and me for Foot Washing Service if we're to save for a reaper. One hundred and twenty-five dollars! It wonders me how we can hope to save half that much."

"Only one way," Martha said, "like Father told us. By all working together." But she did think for a fleeting second that a new bonnet would have been nice.

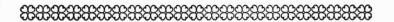

2. TOO MUCH EXCITEMENT

IT WAS not until Friday afternoon, after Father dismissed the twenty students at school, that Martha walked arm in arm along the dirt road with Freda on the way to visit her. Every now and then she gave a little skip, and her eyes were bright. She couldn't help but think how different her own life would be if Father had married a Baptist like Freda's mother. Freda's mother wore a gold wedding ring! Wedding rings were forbidden along with dainty pins, earrings, bracelets, and watches, to Mennonite women.

Mrs. Landis was in the kitchen baking snitz pies when the girls rushed in, and Martha's eyes immediately went to the third finger of her left hand. Yes, the ring was there. She sniffed the delicious smell from the dried apples, or snitz. At home she and Johnny sometimes secretly slipped up to the attic to munch on a few pieces of the dried snitz that hung in strings from the rafters until Mother needed them.

"Umm," Freda said, "may we have some?"

Mrs. Landis smiled at Martha and set plates for them

on the table covered with the same kind of red-checked cloth that Mrs. Sherfey used. Martha tried not to stare at the pin Freda's mother wore at her throat. Freda had told her once it was a cameo, a pin with the silhouette of a lovely lady's head raised above a creamy background.

"So your father is thinking of buying a reaper, not so?" Mrs. Landis asked.

Martha nodded. She had heard Mother say that the entire neighborhood was talking about whether Father would dare go against Grandpa Sherfey. News traveled fast in the country.

The snitz pie was hot and the girls took tiny bites, blowing on each one first. Martha looked around carefully. There was nothing different about the Landis kitchen. It was the parlor that showed the family were not Mennonite.

"Do you still take lessons on the melodeon?" she asked Freda.

Before Freda could reply, her mother said, "Takes lessons she does! But practice she does not! One of these days she will stop taking!"

Freda giggled. "*Ach*, I do practice some! Come in once to hear."

The girls made their way to the parlor and Martha saw it was as elegant as she remembered, with the shades drawn to keep the sun off the soft carpet that had roses woven in it. A Mennonite parlor would have had a rug made from carpet rags. Freda raised the shades and Martha went to look at the fractur on the wall.

Fracturs were handsomely decorated certificates which Pennsylvania Dutch housewives framed for their walls. They could be birth, death, wedding, or baptismal certificates, and for many years itinerant fractur men roamed the countryside, painting and lettering them.

Mrs. Landis' fractur was an old wedding certificate of her grandmother's and Martha loved the design of yellow tulips, pink hearts, trailing vines, and an angel at the top. Some Mennonite families bought fracturs, but strict ministers such as Grandpa frowned on anything that was purely "for fancy."

Martha sighed. It was a disadvantage to have a preacher for a grandfather, and Grandpa hoped Father would follow in his footsteps.

Freda seated herself on the bench in front of the melodeon. She opened a hymnbook and to Martha's delight began to play very softly. The instrument's tone was almost flute-like and to Martha, whose church forbade the use of any musical instrument, the sounds were enchanting.

She stood close to Freda to watch the way she moved her fingers up and down the keyboard, her foot pumping the pedal at the same time. It was like magic. And on one finger Freda wore her gold ring with the red stone.

"Abide with Me" was Freda's favorite, but when she played "Onward, Christian Soldiers," Martha liked the martial way she struck the notes. It made her wonder what it was like in a big church where they used a real organ as an accompaniment for the singing.

"It's getting too dark to see," Freda said finally, and Martha jumped guiltily.

"I'll have to run all the way home. Mother said not to be late. Show me the reaper, quick!"

Catching up their coats and scarfs, the girls ran outside. The reaper stood in a covered shed next to the barn and when Freda explained what her father liked about the machine, Martha understood her father's determination to own one.

It truly was a wonderful thing. Bound sheaves would drop off the platform as the farmer made his way up one row and down another.

"How did your father get so much money all at once?" Martha asked, and then blushed at her forwardness.

"*Ach*," Freda said, "don't you know Cyrus McCormick has sold machinery to farmers this long time? He never makes them pay the whole sum at one time if they can't."

"He doesn't?"

"My father gave thirty-five dollars in cash and paid the freight charges from Chicago."

"You mean he *trusts* you for the balance?" Martha asked in amazement.

Freda nodded, and Martha's excitement mounted within her. She could scarcely wait to tell her parents what she had learned.

"But how can he afford to do such a thing?" she asked.

"He charges interest, like a bank."

That is what Father offered to pay Grandpa, Martha

thought. Interest. Always before the word only meant arithmetic problems, which she hated. For the first time she decided there might be some sense to the subject.

It was almost dark when Martha arrived home, breathless from her run, and she paused momentarily in the kitchen. She would save her news for the supper table.

"After you feed the pigs," Mother said, "you'll find a wheelbarrow load of rotten apples by the cellar door. I want you should dump them for me. Next year I make more snitz and not let so many apples waste."

"A snitz party!" Martha exclaimed. "Can't we have a snitz party? They're more fun than quiltings or husking bees!"

Martha had been to a snitz party at Sarah Moyer's once, and she remembered everyone arriving with aprons and paring knives. Washtubs were loaded with apples, which disappeared rapidly. The apples were sliced into thin strips and laid on cookie sheets for drying in the sun the next day.

Songs were sung as the guests pared and pared and pared. Unmarried girls tried to pare a whole apple without breaking the paring, and when they succeeded, they threw it over their shoulders to see what initial it formed. This was supposed to be that of one's future husband.

With her head in a whirl at the prospect of having a snitz party in their own kitchen, with thoughts of the news she had for Father concerning the reaper payment, plus scattered recollections of Freda in her pink dress playing the melodeon, Martha went about her chores mechanically.

If only I could have a dress like Freda's for the party next fall! It would be fun to make!

In a short time she had wheeled the rotten apples to the pigpen and dumped them inside it. Then she mixed dry feed with water from the pump and emptied that bucket into the trough.

Back in the kitchen she found Father had finished milking early tonight and was ahead of her. Sentences tumbled out of Martha so fast that the family could not understand her words.

"Wait till we have said Grace," Father said at last, "and then start over again."

Johnny grinned at Martha and she smiled back as they bowed their heads.

"Lord bless this food to our use and us to Thy service," Father said, and after several more sentences he mercifully cut his prayer short. Mother began to serve the potpie, which was one of her specialties. Its delicious aroma filled the kitchen, a blend of home-made noodles which Mother cut into squares and large pieces of tender chicken.

Martha repeated what she had been told by Freda, and Father said, "*Ja,* you are telling the truth. I've heard tell McCormick not only guarantees each machine he manufactures, but that he has a credit system for farmers. His agents set up a payment plan for you."

He stopped talking for a moment and then continued, "I had hoped Grandpa would make me a loan, but since he will not—tomorrow morning early we will go to the city. You will go with me, not so?" he asked Mother.

"To Philadelphia?" Mother gasped. "Never have I been to Philadelphia! Who will stay with the children?"

"I'll go by Godshalks' and see if Granny Godshalk can come. But Debbie and Peter had best be left at Kratzes'."

Godshalks on one side of Sherfeys' farm and Kratzes on the other were always ready to help in an emergency. Certainly a thirty-mile trip was not to be undertaken lightly; it was an emergency. It seemed as though now that Father had made up his mind, he could not wait another twenty-four hours to carry out his plan.

"By gum," Johnny said, "will you go on the steam train?"

Father nodded. "We'll leave the horses in the livery stable at Doylestown. Then after we've done our business we'll stop overnight with Uncle Horace's family in Germantown. They'll be glad to put us up."

"And go to meeting with them Sunday morning?" Mother asked. The Germantown Mennonite Meetinghouse would be wonderful to see, Martha realized, for it was the very first Mennonite church built in America. They were all proud that Germantown was founded by thirteen German families in 1689 when William Penn granted them a charter. That date was one Martha did not find hard to remember.

"I'm afraid not. To get back here at a reasonable time we'll have to catch a morning train."

Martha stared in astonishment, and Mother frowned and bit her lower lip. Never could Martha remember her parents missing a Sunday service. Twice when she had been ill she remained home in bed, but both times Mother left her alone, as she was not considered as sick as all that!

What would Grandpa Sherfey say when the family did not appear at Blooming Glen to hear him preach? Suddenly Martha caught her breath. She and Johnny would be there with Granny Godshalk. This was unnerving, as Grandpa would ask where Mother and Father were. How he would storm!

"What else will you do in the city?" Johnny asked, interrupting Martha's thoughts.

"We might walk a bit downtown before we take the horsecar to Uncle Horace's. Would you like to see Strawbridge and Clothier's store on Second Street?"

"That would be some wonderful," Mother said, her eyes bright with anticipation.

The talk continued all through the disappearance of the dessert of rice pudding filled with juicy raisins, and oatmeal cookies. It was not until Father had left for Godshalks' and Kratzes' and Martha was drying the dishes that Mother thought to ask her if she had emptied the wheelbarrow load of rotten apples.

Martha almost dropped one of Mother's white ironstone plates. For at that moment she realized what she had done. Given rotten apples to Goldie and her entire litter!

Pigs die of "the scours" and they can get it from rotten apples! If our pigs die, most likely Father won't be able to buy the reaper. *Ach,* what made me such a *dummkopf?*

She turned her back to Mother and slowly put away the plates. I was thinking of Freda, her so pretty dresses, her gold ring and her mother's pin, the melodeon in the parlor and the fractur on the wall! I didn't think what I was doing for all.

Slowly she hung the dish towel to dry. I can't tell Mother what I did. She trusted me to take good care of Goldie and her pigs. If they die, I'm to blame.

She saw that Mother was so concerned with her own plans she had failed to notice Martha's frightened silence.

I-yi-yi-yi!

3. TROUBLE AT THE BARN

It took Martha so long to go to sleep that when she did drop off she slept soundly and did not hear Mother and Father at half after four. That was the hour when they dressed. Mother prepared breakfast while Father milked, and then they bundled Debbie and Peter into blankets for the carriage ride to Kratzes'.

When Martha opened her eyes the sun was streaming into her bedroom window and her first thought was of the pigs. If they were ill, surely Father would have noticed and not gone to the city. Taking heart, Martha hastily jumped out of bed.

But then she admitted to herself that Father would have no reason to look into the pigpen. The pigs were her responsibility and, like Mother, he trusted her.

Johnny was eating cold shoofly pie when she raced down to the kitchen. He loved pie for breakfast and shoofly with its crisp crust, gooey molasses filling, and luscious crumb top was his favorite.

"Johnny! What do you think I did last night? Gave

the pigs those rotten apples!" Martha watched Johnny's stare of unbelief and then of fright. He understood what the consequences could be.

With one accord the pair grabbed their coats from the hooks by the door and headed for the barn. It seemed to take much longer than usual to run across the space between the two buildings.

Shep, the Sherfeys' collie, leaped beside them, thinking they wanted to play, but they ignored him. At the barn door they paused a moment and Martha held her hand on the latch. She was too frightened to enter.

They listened for the sound of the pigs. If they were well, they would be grunting noisily for feed. But the only sounds they heard were the clucking of the hens in the chicken house nearby and a low moo from Bessie in the field beyond.

"I don't hear them," Martha whispered.

"Come on!" Johnny said, and he raised Martha's hand so that the door swung open.

Inside the dark shadow of the barn the sweet fragrance of hay came to Martha as she made her way to the pen at the back. She loved the smell and usually stopped to sniff a moment. But now she failed to notice it. Two black kittens played about on the floor. She usually stopped to pet them, but today she did not see them.

When she reached the pen Martha took a deep breath and balled her hands together in two tight fists. She stood close to Johnny to peer over the high fence.

Goldie was in the far corner nudging a small black-

and-white piglet Martha had named Spotty. She saw at once that Spotty was having trouble standing. His back legs seemed weak, and Martha saw with a shock that he looked what Grandpa called "mopey."

"They've got it bad, Johnny."

"Look at those by the trough."

Martha saw that instead of noisily shoving each other as they usually did, the pigs were weak and wobbly, with half-closed eyes.

"*Ach*, eleven baby pigs plus Goldie are a big investment. Eight or more of them Father plans to sell come fall. Some of that money could go toward the reaper!" Martha's face grew pale and her lower lip trembled.

Pork roasts, bacon, ham, spareribs, scrapple, lard, sausage—a whole list of meats ran through her mind and left her shivering. How could she have been so thoughtless?

Suddenly she got a grip on herself. There must be something she could do. An idea slowly began to form in her mind.

"Johnny, Grandpa made pap out of boiled milk and flour when his pigs had scours. We'll try it. When Granny comes she'll help us. But we can't wait for her."

"Let's hurry."

Back in the house Martha put kindling into the range to make a hot fire. Then she measured flour from the flour bin that was built into the kitchen cabinet. Johnny went to the cellarway and rolled in the big milk can Father had filled with morning's milk.

"We'll boil the milk in a bucket," Martha said, and when Johnny had almost filled one they lifted it carefully onto the stove.

It took forever for the milk to come to a boil. While Martha mixed in the flour, Johnny brought more kindling. A second bucket was left on the stove to heat.

At the barn the pigs were even more listless, and Martha's knees began to tremble. She wished Granny Godshalk would come to give them a hand. Where was she? She should have arrived by this time. Even though she hated to have Granny know of her carelessness, still she wanted her help.

Johnny opened the gate to the pen and he and Martha stepped in. The pigs ignored them, huddling together, blinking their tiny pink eyes sleepily. Spotty fell down and lay still.

Martha poured the pap into the trough and Goldie planted her two front feet into it and snuffled. But the baby pigs showed little interest in the mixture.

Martha brought Spotty from the corner and pushed his snout into the pap. Spotty kicked feebly and turned his head away. Finally he opened his mouth and took a few swallows. Then he refused to take more.

"Make the ones that have not eaten take some," Martha begged Johnny. "Goldie's getting the most and she's not so sick as the others."

"How long will it take to work?"

"I don't know. Grandpa was up till way late at night when his pigs had it."

"If they're going to die, then we'll know before Father and Mother get home tomorrow," Johnny said.

"Johnny! Don't say such a thing."

"But look at them. Even Goldie's droopy."

Goldie now had returned to the far corner of the pen to settle on the ground. Her mammoth size seemed suddenly to have shrunk and Martha saw she was breathing in great heaves.

"Do you think I put in the right amount of flour and milk?" Martha asked. "I used about a third flour and two thirds milk."

"You're learning some use for arithmetic," Johnny said, and Martha knew he was trying to cheer her up, so she managed a smile.

"I think I'll try half and half. That ought to bring them around if anything will."

"Do you think we could use a bottle of painkiller?"

"Father bought some from the vet, but I'd be scared to try." She pushed her braids back distractedly. "Grandpa said he didn't like to dope his pigs."

"*Ja*, but some died. And they were bigger than Spotty."

" 'Size alone is not enough, else a cow could catch a rabbit,' " Martha quoted. "That's what Granny Godshalk says. Oh, I wish she'd come!"

"When do we feed them again?"

"I think Grandpa fed the pap every hour till they—well, died or got better."

While they were walking across the barnyard Martha remembered that Johnny had forgotten the chickens. She could hear them clucking.

"See how one thing leads to another!" she exclaimed. "Now the hens won't lay so many eggs for Mother!"

So Johnny hurried to the chicken house while she returned to the kitchen. The fire had died and the milk was cold. She set to work again and by the time Johnny joined her the fire was roaring up the stovepipe.

"Wherever do you think Granny is?" she asked at once, and moved to peer through the kitchen window. Right then they heard the sound of buggy wheels up the road. When the carriage came in sight, Martha saw Granny hunched on the seat and she told herself that now things might go better.

But instead of turning into the yard, Granny drove to the front gate. Martha and Johnny raced out the kitchen door and around to the front of the house.

"Say!" Granny began (Granny always began a conversation with "Say!" Father said), "I just got word that Emma Rosenberger up Dublin way is sick with pneumonia. They want me right away. You two hop in and I'll drop you by your grandpa's. You can stay there and he can come milk for your pa tonight."

Martha and Johnny glanced quickly at each other. Almost with one accord they said, "To Grandpa's we can walk. You don't need to wait for us."

Granny looked surprised and stared at them almost suspiciously.

Martha added, "We—we still have things to do b-b-before we can go."

"Too cold it won't be for you to walk such a ways?" Granny asked after a moment. "You think?"

Martha shook her head vigorously, and before either she or Johnny knew what was happening, Granny gave her horse a slap with the reins and she was off. They watched the carriage disappear down the road, no longer able to see Granny's figure as she had the falling top up.

"*Ach*, now we've done it," Johnny said. "Granny could have helped if we'd told."

"Or we could have brought Grandpa right back here." Martha's voice shook. "But, oh, Johnny, I'd have such a shamed face."

Together they turned toward the house.

"Let's get that pap," Martha said. "My fault it was the pigs got the scours. I've got to save them!"

4. A BUSY WEEKEND

THE pigs looked no better when Martha and Johnny returned to the pen, but as Martha tried to convince herself, they looked no worse either. It was only by shoving them into the trough and coaxing patiently that they drank any pap at all.

Johnny brought two milking stools to the pen and he and Martha sat down to watch.

"I'm not going to move till it's time to bring the next bucket," Martha declared.

It was strangely quiet. Maud and May always stamped their feet and snorted at each other, or gave forth an occasional whinny. But now the horses were in the livery stable in Doylestown. Martha could faintly hear the cows breathing and moving in their stalls. Once Goldie gave a loud grunt, and Martha jumped.

She rested her elbows on her knees, her chin in her hands. The barn was cold and after some time she shivered. She tucked her hands into her coat sleeves, wishing she had put on mittens.

"I guess I should have told Granny," Martha said at last. She was stiff and cramped.

"She'd have had to give up going to Rosenbergers'," Johnny answered. "And if Emma has pneumonia— well, Granny's needed there most."

Time crawled by. Martha's eyes burned from staring so hard at the pigs. Some of them lay close to Goldie, but made no attempt to nurse.

"If we go to Grandpa's later we'll have to tell why Father went to the city," Martha said.

"We could stay alone. Nothing worse can happen than already has, unless the pigs die. Could you milk? I can do one cow."

Martha nodded. She never had milked more than one cow, but she would rather milk all three than face Grandpa with the joint news about the pigs and Father's trip to buy a reaper. Without further discussion it was decided. In silence they went to the house.

The clock's hands showed it was noon, but neither suggested they eat. Martha could not remember a time when Johnny did not want food. She wondered if he were saying a silent prayer as she was.

I suppose Father will punish me not only for being careless, but for not going to Grandpa's. But nothing could make me feel worse than I do now!

One o'clock. Two o'clock. Then with the three-o'clock feeding, miraculously the pigs shoved each other and grunted noisily. Goldie swung her big rump so that she crowded Spotty out, and Spotty scooted under her into the trough.

Oink. Oink. The pigs lapped the last of the pap and looked for more. Martha's eyes stung.

Back in the kitchen Johnny threw kindling into the range and Martha brought out leftover potpie to heat on top of the stove. She opened a jar of chowchow, a favorite of Johnny's, and bread-and-butter pickles for herself. There were slices of Mother's bread to eat with apple jelly.

"How about having more shoofly for dessert?" Martha's eyes twinkled. "Would you care for that?"

"I don't care if I do," Johnny replied, and they laughed. This was a saying of the Sherfeys', stemming from a story of Father's about a Doylestown farmer who played tricks on people.

"One time," Father had said, "he was driving along the road and passed a man who was walking. He stopped his horse and buggy and leaned out.

" 'Would you care for a lift?' he asked.

"The man looked up and said, 'I don't care if I do.'

"Just as he was about to step into the carriage the farmer said, 'Well, if you don't care, neither do I!' and drove right on, leaving the man standing there."

And ever after that when anyone asked if they cared for anything, Martha or Johnny always replied, "I don't care if I do."

"If Bessie had freshened we'd have four cows to milk,"

Martha said when she emptied her last bucket into the big milk can that evening. She had scalded the can carefully just as Mother always did and she remembered to put clean cheesecloth over the top so that the milk was strained and clean.

It was eight o'clock by the time they ate supper, and Martha was so tired she ached. But the chores were done. The coal-oil lamp hanging from the ceiling cast a glow over Shep, curled on one of Mother's rag rugs. Whenever there was the sound of horses' hoofs or carriage wheels, Shep raised his head to listen.

"Let's go to bed as soon as the dishes are done," Johnny said. "I'll give you a hand."

Martha knew he was as nervous as she was for fear Grandpa or a neighbor might drop by and find them alone. The sausage cakes, mashed potatoes, bread and pork gravy, applesauce and cold milk tasted good, but nothing would ever taste as good as their first meal after they knew the pigs were safe.

Shep followed them upstairs and took his accustomed place in the hall. Martha decided he did not know what to make of their being alone.

"*Ach,*" she said, "I'm too tired to stay awake worrying how Father will punish me."

Early morning found Martha milking again, and by the time she had finished she was starved. She began to appreciate the amount of cooking Mother did daily. So she fried eggs and bacon, made hot cocoa and toast.

Johnny cut the bacon, trying not to get the slices thin at one end and thick at the other.

"Grandpa will miss us from church," Johnny said.

"Likely he'll think someone sick and come by." Martha dunked her toast in her cocoa the way Father dunked doughnuts in coffee. "I hope Mother and Father are home before he comes!"

"By gum, I do, too!"

"It's the Dutch in him makes Grandpa pinch pennies, Grandma says. Remember how she wanted to give Mother her second-best love seat and a rocker for the parlor? Grandpa wouldn't let her. He said giving folks things makes life too easy for them."

"What was that story Grandpa always tells about the man who got help from his neighbors to feed his family?"

Martha laughed. "Grandpa always tells that when he has hired help at the table, pointing out the man's laziness.

"One day when they were making hay, this lazy man took a nap in the haymow. The men picked him up and threw him into the hay wagon. Then they drove off down the road. As they jogged along they met another wagon and stopped to talk to the driver, telling him they had this worthless one who would not work to feed his family.

"But the driver felt sorry for the man's family and said, 'I'll give him a load of corn.'

"Right then the man sat up to ask, 'Is it shelled?' "

Johnny grinned. "You tell a story just like Father."

Martha's face flushed at the compliment. "I wish I were more like Father," she said, "but I'm not really responsible, Johnny. What do you think Father will say to me?" This was a thought she could not put from her mind.

"*Ach,* don't worry about it. What for does it do any good?"

To pass the time more quickly Martha helped Johnny gather eggs. Although the chickens knew them perfectly well, they flew about and made a fuss when forced to give up their newly laid eggs.

"Hush now, Biddy," Martha repeated over and over.

"Some hens don't care where they lay," Johnny said, retrieving eggs from the straw on the floor.

"Mostly they like to be in the dark." Martha dropped the burlap curtains over one row of wooden boxes.

A red rooster with a gorgeous tail ran about frantically. Sometimes he pecked Johnny and then Johnny teased him until the rooster strutted away, crowing loudly.

For noon dinner Martha knew Granny Godshalk would have killed an old hen, stewed her, and made dumplings, so she looked the hens over carefully. There was a trick to choosing one that was not laying well. Finally she recalled Mother saying a hen that was not laying had a pale comb.

Having decided on the luckless hen, Martha carried

her upside down by her legs to the chopping block. She never had killed a fowl before, but she had seen Mother do it many times. The ax was sharp and she knew she must be careful not to cut herself as Johnny had when he first chopped kindling.

"Can you do it?" Johnny asked. He did not like the sight of blood and always made himself scarce when it was time for this job. Now Martha supposed he did not know whether to stand by to lend support or not.

"I guess so." Martha took a piece of cord Mother kept handy and tied the hen's legs tightly together and then laid her sidewise on the block. She took the ax in her right hand and made testing motions up and down near

the chicken. Then, suddenly closing her eyes, she brought the ax down in one fell swoop. It was better luck than management, she admitted afterward, for she might have struck the chicken anywhere else than the neck.

"I'm glad I remembered to tie her legs," she said, "or she'd flap all over the place even though she is dead."

Johnny brought a bucket of scalding water and Martha dunked the hen's body. After it was well soaked she and Johnny stripped off the feathers. It was a messy but not a difficult task.

Then back in the kitchen Martha cleaned out the insides with a sharp knife. She was proud she did not break the gall, which would turn the chicken bitter.

All the time she worked, however, she thought about whether she should tell Mother that she was thinking of pink dresses, gold rings, cameos, and melodeons when she gave the pigs the rotten apples. That truly was the worst part of her action.

While the chicken stewed gently on the stove she made dough for the dumplings and shredded a head of cabbage for slaw.

"No wonder Mother's so busy," she said to Johnny. "She always says she's up to her ears in work and the wrong way in at that."

They both talked a lot in an effort to keep from thinking of the church service they had missed and what Granny Godshalk might have said to Grandma and Grandpa Sherfey.

Dinner was not ready till after three o'clock, and by

that time they were both listening nervously for Grandpa's carriage.

At last they heard carriage wheels and Shep barked a joyful greeting. Martha sighed with relief. Father and Mother had arrived first!

The next ten minutes were a blur of excitement as Martha and Johnny both talked at once, explaining why Granny was not with them and all about the pigs. Martha could not bring herself to confess what had made her forgetful.

"I-yi-yi-yi, you mean you two stayed here all night alone?" Mother asked.

"And recovered the pigs are? Every last one?" Father interrupted.

Then he went directly to the pigpen to check before he unharnessed Maud and May and put away the carriage. Meanwhile Martha helped Mother take off Debbie's things and fix Peter.

"See what I brought," Mother said later. She opened a package and took out a small piece of flowered material. "Just enough for a bonnet for you for Foot Washing Service. A remnant it was, or I could not have afforded it."

Martha touched the material gently. There were bright pink roses and pale yellow roses on a white background. Never had she seen such a pretty piece. To think that Mother spared the money and she herself had almost lost the family's pigs!

"*Ach*, but it's too pretty, yet," Martha said.

Then there was another small piece for Mother's own bonnet. This was black satin. A satin dress would be too worldly, but Mother had decided to risk the bonnet.

"A pink rose I wanted," she explained, "to go on this, but then I knew that talk it would cause. Such a pretty rose it was."

Martha looked at Mother in silence. So she, too, yearned for the things that were considered fancy. She would understand if she told her of her thoughts when she fed the pigs.

But at that moment Grandpa's carriage drove into the yard and Mother's face paled. Johnny burst in the door, saying unnecessarily, "Here's Grandpa."

"Better you children should go upstairs a little while," Mother said. "Take Debbie with you."

Glad to escape, Martha and Johnny left the room immediately. Martha dreaded the thought of Grandpa's anger at her disobedience. But then he might be so furious at Father that he would be distracted from thinking of her.

"Shall we listen?" Johnny asked in a whisper.

Debbie hung back, but Martha took her hand firmly and pulled her on.

"Let's anyhow not," Martha said. "Enough trouble we've been in, not so?"

Up in her room she sang Debbie to sleep to make it impossible to hear the talk that went on below.

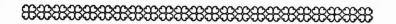

5. A BEAD RING

THERE was little talk at the Sherfeys' of anything except the reaper during the next week. Father had ordered it for delivery just before the wheat harvest. What Grandpa had said Martha did not know.

But Joe Godshalk and Jake Kratz had come by to hear about it and Father showed them the advertisement in the paper. They looked dubious when he talked of its marvels.

Once Martha overheard Father tell Mother, "When the reaper arrives and Grandpa sees how it works, he'll come around."

"*Nein,*" Mother objected. "A hundred and twenty-five dollars is too much money no matter what a machine can do. Change his mind about that you never will!"

Martha whispered to Johnny, "If Sunday were not Foot Washing Service when Grandpa has to preach from the eighteenth chapter of Matthew he would hunt for a text to point up Father's sin of extravagance." This made them both giggle.

Then on Monday night Father brought up Martha's punishment. She was sewing on her brown dress and Mother was cutting out their bonnets. Father spoke quietly. "Martha will not be wearing a new bonnet."

"*Ach*, John," Mother protested, "never will she feed Goldie or any pigs rotten apples again!"

"That I am sure," Father agreed, "but Granny told her to go to Grandpa's. Disobedience must be punished. The pigs we might have lost."

As Martha looked at the lovely pink and yellow roses they blurred before her eyes. She nodded her head, however, for she knew she had been wrong. In fact, she had known it when she listened to Johnny's suggestion that they stay home. But of this punishment she had not dreamed.

Mother said no more, but rose to put the materials away.

"Finish yours," said Father.

"How can I wear it when—" Mother stopped.

"For you I bought it."

Mother and Martha looked at each other, and Martha wished she could live over last weekend. Mother would grieve over her punishment.

So each night that week Martha sewed, taking tiny stitches and trying not to tell herself that if the dress were pink she would like making it. Continual rebellion against their Mennonite ways kept her in a turmoil.

Why don't I learn after what happened when I was feeding the pigs? Why am I so full of crazy notions?

Crazy notions was what Sarah Moyer called Martha's yearnings. Martha spent an entire lunch period telling Sarah the story of her visit to Freda's house. They sat together on a long bench at the back of the schoolroom, Sarah's eyes wide.

"Next thing you know," Sarah said, her tone of voice showing her amazement at Martha's heresy, "you'll think it nice for a woman to wear that thing they call a bustle."

"What's a bustle?"

"Granny Godshalk told about it last Sunday after meeting. She said there's a woman at the Baptist church at Nace's Corner who wears one. It's like a little hoop just in the back and makes your, well, your *whatever* stick out!"

Martha laughed. "What else did Granny say?"

"She said, 'Say! Do you know when this here woman went to climb into the buggy she lifted up her skirt to arrange that bustle and men saw her ankles!' "

Sarah was eating a piece of Funny Cake and she exchanged half of it for a piece of Martha's Funeral Pie. Funny Cake is piecrust filled with melted chocolate and cake, while Funeral Pie is raisin pie.

"I wonder will Freda's mother have a bustle?" Martha asked, her mouth full of raisins. "It would be some easier to be a Baptist, not so?"

"It's unscriptural to marry out of the church." Sarah paused to lick some chocolate from her fingers.

When they finally exhausted the subject of Freda's clothes, the parlor with its melodeon and fractur, Sarah said, "About your father ordering a reaper everyone is talking."

"I guess some think it good and some are like Grandpa and say it is foolish to spend money for such a machine. What does your father say?"

"He approves. But he said it would take awhile to bring the old men around. A preacher like your grandfather makes folks listen."

Martha nodded seriously. Folks would listen to him this Sunday after service even if Grandpa could not preach his sermon about Father's extravagance. Ministers such as Grandpa were selected for definite qualifications as set forth in the Bible. They had no formal training. Martha could recite First Timothy 3:1–13 and Titus 1:6–9 stating the kind of men they must be.

Just to herself Martha smiled at one phrase, "Not self-willed." She recalled the verse that said a bishop should rule his own house, having his children under subjection, or he could not rule the House of God. Father said it had been Grandpa's ruling with an iron hand that kept them living with him for thirteen years!

"Mother plans on having a quilting so the women can come with the men on the day Father harvests," she told Sarah now. "Will you all come? The reaper will be delivered early in July."

Sarah's eyes twinkled. "Father said he wouldn't miss it for a ticket to the Fair!"

Both girls laughed, as fairs were forbidden also, but many a Mennonite boy sneaked away and visited a carnival or a sideshow before he settled down as a good husband. Martha thought it was very unfair that girls were unable to try such things. If she ever had a chance to do something the boys could—she would!

"Do you have a quilt to go in the frame?" Sarah wanted to know.

"*Nein*. You know, sewing I hate. But my dress is almost ready for Sunday."

Then Father rang the bell to end the lunch period. Boys and girls raced in, breathless from exercise.

The twenty pupils ranged in age from six to nineteen. Older boys came only during the winter because they worked in the fields the rest of the year.

Few girls attended after they were thirteen. People thought that girls only needed to learn to read and write as they would marry early. Father gave each student whatever work he or she could do.

Little ones who could speak only Pennsylvania Dutch or German learned English first. The smarter boys learned a smattering of Latin and read Shakespeare. Those in between had the three R's. There were no grades, but students were divided into five classes.

When Father sent Martha to the blackboard to do problems she shook so it was difficult to make the numbers straight and even. If the answer was not correct, she would have to go over it again and again until she found the right answer.

"Why must I learn arithmetic?" she whispered to Sarah when she returned to her desk. It was a seat near the window and too often she sat looking out at the trees and sky, dreaming away the minutes she should have spent more profitably.

"When I grow up I'll never, never, never do another problem!"

"*Ja*, but you will." Sarah laughed at her. "To Doylestown you'll go to shop and have to count your money to not be cheated. What if you don't know how many feet in a yard? For making dresses, how can you buy goods?"

"Oh, counting I can do. But fractions or per cent, or square root, that gets me all *verhuddled*. But girls can't work when they're grown unless they hire out on a farm, so what good to learn?"

"Maybe you'll teach school."

"*Nein*, hardly any women teach. And when they marry, that is the end of it."

"Better to marry than be an old maid," Sarah said. "Look at the aunt that I'm named after. No husband she has, so she lives with one relative and then another. She does all the mending at each place and wears somebody's hand-me-down dresses. That's not going to happen to me!"

Johnny and Matt, Sarah's brother, sitting side by side in front of Sarah, hooted derisively and then choked off their noise when Father looked up from his desk at the front of the room. He was hearing the smaller ones read from McGuffey's First Reader and the children sat in a row on a benching facing him.

Martha smiled at Sarah's statement. She knew Sarah was "laying things by" for her dower chest. Sarah could make as fine a pillowcase or hem a sheet as neatly an any woman. Martha supposed she should be doing the same thing. Even if you did not marry till you were eighteen, it took a long while to make enough linens.

But there again—how she hated plain things and having to sew them! A pillowcase with fancy embroidery, or crocheted tidies for the back and arms of a horsehair settee might be fun to make. And just imagine growing up and having to marry and always sew black dresses for best. Never in her whole life would she be able to see how she looked in a gay pink or soft blue.

Freda's even got a red alpaca for best in wintertime. It makes your spirits lift just to look at it, with lace on the collar and on the white cuffs.

So Tuesday, Wednesday, and Thursday went by. It was on Thursday night that Martha found the tiny red beads in Mother's wooden sewing box. She had gone for more thread and for the first time noticed a small envelope lying on the bottom. When she looked inside and saw the beads, she caught her breath. They would decorate a brown dress if you could make a design at the neck. But she knew this would be frowned upon.

Slowly she sifted the beads back and forth through her hands. They were very old beads, probably some that her mother had received from her own mother and never been allowed to use. Then an idea came to her.

Suppose she strung a few of the beads on a thread and tied it into the shape of a ring? In the summer she and Sarah often made necklaces and bracelets of daisy chains.

There's not enough beads for a necklace or bracelet, she thought, but a ring—that would be possible.

Without further thought Martha cut a piece of button thread, made a knot, and began slipping beads on it. When she had finished, she tried it on, and although it did not compare with Freda's gold ring with the red stone, still it was a pretty thing. But she did not dare keep it on her finger, so she slid it into her apron pocket.

I'll wear it to bed tonight. And sometimes maybe put it on for an hour or so to show Sarah at school.

And so she did. Sometimes she took it out and looked at it when she was sure no one could see her. It was such a gay little thing. What harm could there be in wearing it?

The following day, just before noon recess, she slipped it on her finger. And when she and Sarah were sitting close together eating their lunch, suddenly Sarah spied it. While she exclaimed over it, Freda came over. She admired it also, and before Martha knew exactly what was happening Emma Kratz and two other girls joined them. There was considerable ohing and ahing.

Suddenly a voice inquired quietly: "What have we here?"

The words froze Martha; they were her father's. He had come upon them before she realized he had re-

entered the room. Her heart did a complete somersault and for a moment stopped beating.

"I made it," she said, her voice scarcely above a whisper. "The beads were in Mother's sewing box."

"I see," he said. "This we will talk of later."

Martha slid the ring back into her apron pocket where she could feel it all the rest of the day and wish that she had not been so tempted.

Father said nothing further until late that evening when she again was sewing on her dress. She was finishing the hem now and all that remained to do was to press it.

"Get the Bible, Martha," Father said.

Mother and Johnny looked up and Martha avoided their glances. Father did not explain, but Martha understood at once what he meant her to read.

When she had placed the big Bible on the kitchen table Father said, "Read aloud Second Timothy, the ninth and tenth verses."

Slowly Martha read the directive which she knew by heart. Women should dress themselves in modest apparel, "not with broidered hair, or gold or pearls or costly array, but which becometh women professing godliness with good works."

"You may keep the ring," Father said, "not to wear, but to remind you of your weakness. Put it in a box in your bureau drawer. And whenever you want something fancy—open the box. It will be a symbol for you."

"I should have given the beads away or gotten rid of them long ago," Mother said. "They were my mother's and so pretty I put them in the sewing box years ago and forgot they were there. Someday you also will forget."

Martha said nothing. Somehow this time the fact that Mother had wanted much the same things as she wanted did not help. She was sure now that never would she be reconciled to dressing plain.

6. A BUGGY RACE

SUNDAY mornings always were a rush. They slept later than usual, so that when Father finished milking he came back to the house on the run. Mother was flying around the kitchen apparently doing six things at once. She was frying ham and its salty smell made Martha sniff hungrily. Johnny was amusing Peter to keep him quiet.

Martha set the table and buttoned Debbie up the back. Mother plaited Martha's hair to be sure it was as neat as possible, with no ends sticking out as they sometimes did when she took care of it herself.

"I won't dress Peter till the last minute," Mother said. "My, but I'm glad he's out of long dresses and into short ones."

So it went right through breakfast and the clearing away of the dishes. Then Mother browned a pot roast in her iron Dutch oven and set it on the back of the stove so it would be ready when they returned from meeting. Martha pared the potatoes and cried over peeling the onions that were to be cooked with it.

"Put a spoon in your mouth," Mother advised, "or you'll have red eyes from crying when we get to service."

Even though they were going to church they had their family worship service after breakfast in the dining room. Each morning Father prayed for guidance when the Sherfeys had their worship service. Should he go against Grandpa's wishes when Grandpa was one of the ministers of the Blooming Glen Mennonite Church?

Worship was held in the dining room because the parlor lacked furniture. The dining room had a big, round oak table and a tremendous buffet from Mother's old home, and there were six straight chairs with flowers painted on the rung across the back of each. All the years they lived at Grandpa's the dining-room pieces had been stored in the carriage shed.

It seemed to Martha they never would be ready to leave, but finally they were off. Mother in her new bonnet was on the front seat of the carriage, holding Peter, and Debbie sat between Mother and Father. Martha and Johnny were on the back seat. The day was warm and sunny so that they did not need to wrap in blankets and the carriage was open without any side curtains for protection.

"I'm glad we don't need hot bricks to warm our feet today," said Martha. In winter it was her job to warm the bricks in the oven and wrap them in pieces of old quilts to carry outside. She happily gave a small bounce on the seat. It could not be a very big one, because she knew she must sit decorously on the way to service.

The best part of going to church was the ride. Today Father had tied a strand of red silk into Maud's and May's tails for good luck and they looked very handsome. Martha thought he needed good luck today. How would Grandpa greet them?

As they drove along Mother commented on the maple trees that had budded out since last Sunday, the lawns that were turning green, the families that already had whitewashed their picket fences, and the new hex signs on Kratzes' barn. Grandma Sherfey believed hex signs kept the witches away—some were five-pointed stars and others were circular designs.

When they passed another buggy, Mother nodded politely and Martha did the same, if they knew the folks only slightly. But if it were someone like Granny Godshalk and Joe, or the Kratz family, with Frank and Emma dressed in their Sunday best and looking more scrubbed than ever, they waved.

Martha kept looking ahead down the road, because if the Moyers came out of their lane while the Sherfeys were in sight, Martha knew her father and Mr. Moyer would race. Sam Moyer had a pair of matched grays he had bought at a sale last year. He had paid a lot more money for them than Father had for Maud and May, so when Father beat him now and then, he was delighted.

"Now, John," Mother said as she always did, "if we see the Moyers, no racing. Your father will only have something more to talk about if you do when we pull into the churchyard."

"Might as well be hung for a sheep as a lamb!" Father grinned at her sideways. "Grandpa raced when he was young, not so?"

Martha wondered if Father really felt so spunky. If Grandpa was so angry he would not speak to them, that would cause talk among folks. There was sure to be a discussion of the reaper after service, with the men taking sides.

"It's Communion Sunday, for all," Mother was protesting. "This once you might listen to me."

"*Ach*, did you hear what Nace's hired men did last Saturday night?" Father asked.

Martha and Johnny stifled giggles. Momentarily Martha forgot her worry. The best part of Father's stories was that they were true. And when Father told them Martha and Johnny could clearly picture what had happened.

Martha knew he was relating this one so Mother would stop talking about how he should not race Mr. Moyer. He would get her mind away from this, and then if the Moyer carriage appeared he would suddenly flourish his whip and they would be off.

"*Nein*," Mother murmured, and her lips twitched almost as though she suspected Father's motive.

"Well," he began, "it seems their barn is overrun with rats. Old Man Nace said he'd pay the men to catch a bunch of them, so to the barn the men went with clubs. They sat on a table he has out there and every time a rat darted out of a hole a man went for it.

"About a hundred they killed that night, and then someone got the idea to tie them by their tails to a rope. They strung the rope between the fence posts at the head of Detweiler's lane and when Henry drove out to church next morning he couldn't get onto the road. He had to take the dead rats down and dispose of them first!"

Mother shuddered at this tale, but Johnny nudged Martha. There ahead of them was the Moyer lane and just making the turn onto the road was their buggy. Father saw it, too, and with a sudden slap of the reins he increased Maud's and May's gait from a sedate trot to a long, loping gallop. Martha grabbed the seat and hung on tightly.

Mother caught hold of her bonnet with one hand and held Peter tightly with the other. Debbie squealed and sat up straight in the seat so she could see better. Even Debbie knew what was taking place.

No one spoke. Father leaned forward and whispered in a coaxing voice to the mares.

"Atta girl, Maud. Step out there, May!"

To Martha it seemed as though the horses understood him perfectly. Down the road they went in an effort to catch the grays and pass them. Martha saw Sarah's father lean out to look back. He waved his whip and Father waved back.

Faster and faster went the horses, and the carriage swayed wildly when they rounded a curve. Suddenly they hit a thank-you-ma'am, and the unexpected dip took Martha's breath.

Finally it seemed as if they were gaining, and as they reached the outskirts of Blooming Glen the road widened and Father took advantage of this. Maud and May put on a last spurt and Father pulled up beside the Moyers' carriage.

Martha looked across and saw that Sarah's mother was clutching the baby just as Mother held tightly to Peter. Sarah and Matt were rolling on the back seat from one side to the other as the light carriage swung almost into the ditch.

But the Sherfeys could not pass this time. So the two buggies flew down Main Street side by side and right into the churchyard, where the horses came to a sudden

stop by the carriage sheds. People in the yard scurried
out of the way and those on the church porch paused to
see who was racing in.

"I-yi-yi-yi," Mother said, "you'll be the death of me
yet." She straightened her bonnet and waited for Father
to come around and help her down.

Martha and Sarah, Johnny and Matt grinned at each
other without saying a word. As the men led the horses
into the shed, Martha saw her mother give Sarah's
mother a smiling look that she felt said plainly, "*Ach,
men!*"

Suddenly Martha was perplexed. She moved close to

Sarah and whispered, "Isn't it queer that Mennonite men love horse racing and can buy handsome animals to pull their buggies? Isn't that having something fancy? It wonders me!"

Sarah did not answer, but Martha had to smile because she looked so scandalized. Somehow Sarah never had these crazy notions.

As they entered the church Mother carried Peter, and Martha followed, holding Debbie's hand. They hung their bonnets and coats on hooks on the women's side of the church. Most of the women wore shawls instead of coats. Then from the box reserved for each one on a shelf above the hooks they lifted down their tiny net prayer caps.

There was no mirror for Martha to look into as she settled the cap on her soft brown hair. That would have been vanity. But when she first had the cap after joining the church she had looked into the mirror in her bedroom. She did not think it hid her hair, but made it really look very nice!

There were so many glances in her direction that Martha guessed Granny Godshalk had told of her not going to Grandpa's and of how she let the pigs get the scours. Her face began to burn.

Sunshine whitened the walls as it poured through the large, clear glass windows evenly spaced down the sides of the building, and the kerosene lamps hanging from the ceiling were so brightly polished they seemed to give off sparks.

Martha could see Grandma Sherfey up front in the very first pew. Grandpa, being one of the two ministers, was on the platform.

So, Martha thought, Grandpa was not out front to see Father and Sam Moyer racing. She glanced toward Mother to see if she might be noticing this. But Mother seemed as calm as usual.

Now there was the Communion Service and the Foot Washing to go through, and then they would find out what Grandpa would say to Father about the reaper in front of folks. Maybe it was just as well she had not been allowed to wear a bonnet with pink and yellow roses. Grandpa would take note of it and snort to Father, "A fool and his money are soon parted. Like father, like daughter."

She saw Grandpa nod his head briefly in Father's direction. All feuds are supposed to be forgotten on Communion Sunday, at least, Martha thought, till after service.

7. GRANDPA IS ANGERED

THE Communion Service was first, and Grandpa preached from Matthew 18 as Martha and Johnny had known he would. He chose the third verse, "Except ye be converted, and become as little children, ye shall not enter into the kingdom of heaven."

For a few minutes Martha managed to listen to his words, and then her attention wandered. Church was an ideal place to dream. It was better than when she sat in school, because there Father called on her to recite or do a problem on the board.

She noticed which women had new bonnets hanging on the hooks. Grandma Sherfey was not one of them, but Sarah's mother's and Mrs. Kratz's were new. Then she studied Sarah's new gray dress and decided that it was no more neatly made than her own. She felt satisfied that she had accomplished something worth while, even if she did not like it!

Grandpa talked and talked. Mothers holding babies

rocked them gently back and forth. Peter fell asleep and Mother laid him down on the seat and carefully stretched her arm a bit. Debbie's eyes were growing heavy.

At long last Grandpa stopped, and the second minister's turn came. He chose the twenty-first and twenty-second verses of Matthew 18—where Peter asked Jesus how many times he should forgive a brother who has sinned against him. Martha knew, even before the minister quoted it, that the answer was, "Not seven times, but seventy times seven."

Again she tried to concentrate on the preacher's words. But try as she would her mind wandered. Here and there a baby cried and a mother nursed it. Debbie slept now, and Martha wished she could curl up on the seat beside her.

The Communion Service woke her up and she had the feeling it had given her the first time she was allowed to take part—that now the wrong thing she had done would be forgiven.

When it was time for the Foot Washing Service, Father stepped to the front, struck the tiny tuning fork to give the congregation the pitch, and then led the singing. In perfect harmony, without any accompaniment, they sang,

> "Our Lord when He was here below
> Washed His disciples' feet, we know,
> And then in language clear and meet
> Bade us to wash each other's feet."

This was such a clear order that Martha wondered why all churches did not do this thing. Then she blushed, deciding that other statements in the Bible also were clear, as her father had pointed out to her. But she did not like them.

Bishop Rosenberger and Grandpa Sherfey took off their black coats and tied large white aprons about their waists. Two deacons, coatless and in aprons, went into a room on the right. They brought out backless benches, two for the men's side and two for the women's.

By now Grandpa and Bishop Rosenberger had removed their shoes and stockings and performed for each other this ancient rite of foot washing. Then Martha began to remove her own shoes and stockings. She and Mother waited their turn to go up the aisle, watching the deacon's wives serving the women.

It was a very solemn ceremony, and Martha felt a little tingle of happiness when it was over. On their way back to their pew Mother paused to kiss Grandma Sherfey and Sarah's mother. Martha kissed Grandma, too, and then she and Sarah exchanged a light touch on the cheek.

Martha smiled across at Johnny. Next year Johnny would join the church and then he would take part in this service. The men, too, kissed each other lightly if they were close friends, such as Father and Mr. Moyer, or they shook hands.

During the service Martha had forgotten her excitement about what would happen afterward when the families paused to talk on the wide porch. But now as she and her mother with Debbie and Peter joined the group gathered around Grandma, Martha saw the men were crowding around Father. Johnny stood close by and he winked at Martha. She started to move toward him, but Grandma Sherfey stopped her.

"*Ach,*" she said, "I hear tell you fed the pigs rotten apples. That doesn't sound like you."

"She had something on her mind and didn't think yet," Mother said.

"Grandpa and I could have come to help," Grandma continued, and Martha felt her cheeks burn. "Lucky you were this time that they got cured."

"Have you turkey eggs you're not setting?" Mother asked.

"*Ja,* eight of them you're welcome to."

"Martha could put them under a broody hen and let her hatch them. Martha's good at that."

"You have a new bonnet," Grandma commented next as she stared at Mother's head, and now it was Mother's cheeks that flushed.

"A remnant the material was from Strawbridge and Clothier's," said Mother.

What would Grandma say now? Martha held her breath.

After a moment's silence Grandma spoke. "Grandpa told of your trip. He is some put out over the reaper. He is not one to spend foolishly."

"Do you think it foolish?" asked Mother, nervously patting Peter on his back.

Grandma shrugged her plump shoulders. "Well, a

Saturday is not a bad day to make a money investment."

Martha and Mother glanced at each other quickly and hid their smiles. Grandma Sherfey was always careful to do things on the right day. She taught Martha never to plant carrots when there was a new moon, for then they would be fork-rooted. Grandma planted climbers such as beans and peas when the horns of the moon pointed up, and potatoes during the increase of the moon and in the sign of the Lion.

When Grandpa Sherfey had rheumatism, Grandma gave him a horse chestnut to carry in his pocket as a cure. When a cock crowed before midnight, Grandma was positive there would be a death in the family.

"*Ach,* you may say that the day doesn't matter," Grandma went on, "but Grandpa bought a cow at the sale last week on the wrong day and it is *verhexed.* She won't give down her milk when Abe is in the barn. What do you make of that?"

Martha knew what Mother would think—that Grandma did not like Abe, the hired man who replaced Father when the family bought their own farm. Martha guessed Grandma would not say whose side of the reaper argument she was on. She was waiting to see if the machine worked.

Slowly Martha moved nearer to the men's group. It was Grandpa who was speaking.

"We'll have a late frost. This warm weather is unseasonable."

"Too bad that would be," said Father; "it might catch the strawberries."

Oh, no! Martha and Johnny glanced at each other and Martha felt a twinge of fear. If frost harmed her plants, she would not have any money toward the reaper.

"There was a ring around the moon last night," Grandpa went on, "and that foretells snow. It is too late for that—so probably it will frost."

"You were in a bit of a hurry this morning, not so?" Bishop Rosenberger asked Father, and suddenly Martha felt an explosion was coming.

"He's always in a hurry!" Grandpa's voice suddenly thundered, and he shook his finger in Father's direction. "What do you think of such a fool as to buy one of those newfangled reapers?"

"Well, now," Bishop Rosenberger said mildly, "some say they are the coming thing. But seems like a lot of money to me."

"Say!" exclaimed Joe Godshalk, borrowing his wife's pet expression, "there are folks crazy enough to believe someday they'll have a machine go along without horses to pull it. Like the steam trains, maybe."

Everyone laughed.

"*Ach*, well," Bishop Rosenberger agreed, "steam trains and boats without sails are one thing, but reapers without a horse!" He shook his head.

"The day you harvest your wheat with that new contraption I want to see it, John," Joe said.

"You're all invited for a demonstration," Father said.

Grandpa snorted. "Next thing you'll be taking out insurance against your barn being burned like Leidy Hunsicker did. You will get yourself expelled from the church!"

Martha shivered. What did Grandpa mean?

"No, I won't," Father said, "but not because I don't think it a sensible thing. Insurance is something Mennonites never believed in, like not going to war, not using guns, or belonging to fraternal societies; but there is no law that says a man can't buy machinery to improve his farming methods."

"What makes you think such a machine's an improvement?" Jake Kratz inquired. "Likely you'll spend so much time fixing the blamed thing when it breaks down that you could bind the field in the meantime by hand."

"Out west," Father said, "where the farms are bigger than ours, this type of machine is very popular. There were fifty thousand reapers sold right after the new wire binder was invented."

"That wire binder!" Grandpa interrupted. "Bits of wire broke off and got mixed in with the straw and the cattle ate it! What do you think of that? You want your cows to eat wire?"

"This new one is a twine binder, so that can't happen."

"Well, you'll never get it paid for," Grandpa said.

"Never is a long time," said Father.

Father's voice was still low and even, and Martha thought he made more impression on the men than Grandpa did when he ranted on. The crowd gradually was thinning out now and horses and buggies were departing rapidly from the churchyard.

"Come once," Grandma Sherfey called as she waved from their buggy. But Grandpa said nothing.

"We will," Mother answered. "You come, too."

"Let's go," Johnny whispered. "I'm starved. What's for dinner?"

"Pot roast," Mother said. "And if Grandma Sherfey knew I had prepared it on the Sabbath she would be shocked. But there was such a much to do yesterday. Spring housecleaning is a job. And Grandma's through hers already."

Father smiled and spoke to the horses. The carriage rolled out of the churchyard and down the street. They passed the store and the blacksmith's shop, the neat brick houses with wide front porches, and then the brick-yard. At last they were out in the country, the town behind them.

"Father," Martha asked, "how does insurance work?"

"You mean fire insurance on barns? Well, so many barns are struck by lightning in summer that farmers take out insurance. Then if their barn is struck the company pays them so they can build a new one. It is only sensible, but our people forbid any kind of insurance."

"What would happen if our barn burned? How could you build it again without the money to buy materials?" It was a frightening possibility, Martha thought.

"We'd lose the cows and maybe Maud and May," Johnny said.

"I-yi-yi-yi," Mother interrupted, "don't borrow trouble."

"Would we have to live with Grandpa?" Martha asked.

"A man has to save to get ahead, and if bad luck hits him, he has something put aside for his rainy day," Father explained. "That is why Grandpa is careful with his money, you see? But we're just starting out and to get ahead takes time. Once we finish paying for the reaper, we can begin to save a bit, too. The reaper is to make us money. But putting out that much is risky if you have nothing to fall back upon."

Martha looked at her father with new respect. She was sure from what she heard him say to the men that he believed in carrying insurance, but as long as Mennonites forbade this he would obey their laws. And she knew he would hate returning to live with Grandpa more than any of them.

"Sometimes," Father said, "having insurance leads a man into trouble. That is if he is not a strong man and a good one. Did you ever hear the story of Bill Haldeman?"

Martha and Johnny sat forward on the seat to hear the tale.

"Bill was a weak man. He had insurance on his barn. When he got in a tight spot for money, he went out to the barn, lighted a candle, and left it burning in the hay. Then he went away, and by the time the hay took fire he was clear out to Hilltown store. He thought no one would ever know.

"But the insurance company investigated and found out the truth. So he never was paid and he had no barn. Then when the church found out he had carried insurance, he was expelled."

When they turned into their own drive Martha looked at the barn with new eyes. It was in need of fresh red paint and it had no hex signs, but it had a fine stone doorsill and there were stalls for twenty cows. Someday Father would have that many and perhaps more.

Then there was the part of the barn where Maud and May were kept, in addition to the pigpen at the back. And a small room for straining milk and the big haymow —and at one side the carriage shed.

If our barn burned, I'd be bitter! But Father would not. And he'd not be defeated either. But what could he do?

Wanting to wear a bead ring is such a little thing. But wanting to carry insurance to protect your family's living, that is a horse of another color! *Ach,* she thought suddenly, but I hope I make money from my strawberries to help Father.

It was then that Martha remembered Grandpa Sherfey's prediction of frost. Farming was risky. Truly you were dependent on the weather, which you could not control. A feeling of foreboding made her shiver as she climbed down from the carriage to go to the house.

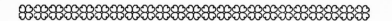

8. GRANDPA WAS RIGHT

MARTHA studied the weather anxiously during the next few days. Each night before she went to bed she looked at the sky, and when she saw a ring around the moon she was worried.

Would Grandpa be right? Father seemed worried, too, which was upsetting.

First thing each morning she jumped out of bed and ran to the window to see if the ground glistened with frost. There was no time before school to run up to the plot of ground where she had worked so hard planting several hundred strawberry plants, covering the rows with straw to mulch them in and keep the weeds down. But the moment she reached home in the afternoon, she raced up the hill.

Perhaps the hill was not a good spot. It was so open to the icy wind that blew down from Haycock Mountain where Father once went lumbering with Levi Nace and his men.

The first three days all was well, but on the third morning the front yard was white and there was a skim of ice on the ground by the pump. Martha's heart sank.

This time without pausing to give Mother a hand setting the breakfast table, dressing Debbie, or feeding Peter, Martha hurried from the house. Mother did not call her back and that was also a bad sign. Clutching her coat rather than stop to button it, she bent her head against the wind and ran breathlessly up the path.

At the top the strawberry bed stretched out before her, hundreds of white blossoms clustered among the dark green leaves. Grandma Sherfey had taught her years ago how to tell if frost had harmed the plants. Grandma raised the biggest and juiciest berries in Bucks County.

Kneeling down, Martha looked for the tiny blossom. She gave way to a sob. A tiny black fleck was visible in the yellow center. That was all she needed to know. The blossoms were frosted.

Slowly she stood up to look over the entire bed. Perhaps some other row might have escaped. For a moment she let hope take its place in her heart.

She moved rapidly from one row to another, searching carefully. But row after row of plants had flowers with the tiny telltale flecks.

Why did this have to happen to her when she wanted so badly to sell a big crop of berries? Now, how could she help Father?

Is this my punishment? Has God punished me because I wanted pretty clothes and fancy jewelry and wished we had a melodeon in the parlor and a fractur on the wall?

All those things I've wished for. Not just one thing, but so many!

Slowly Martha made her way back down the hill. At the barn she fed the pigs without calling to her father, whom she could hear finishing with the cows. Johnny came in from the chicken house as she returned to the kitchen and he looked at her without speaking. Mother must have told him and he knew of no words to comfort her. Johnny would have a calf to contribute, but now what could she do to earn money?

Back in the kitchen Mother spoke at once. "It is no use to cry over spilt milk. There may be enough berries for us to eat. That is something."

"Did it happen because—because I like fancy things and want them yet?"

"*Nein,*" Mother protested. "God is just and kind. He is like a father to us and He does not punish us for our weakness in such things. He knows it is hard to give up the worldly things we would like to have.

"Other folks will have been hit by the frost, not so? Joe Godshalk's peach trees more than likely are touched. They're high, too. We hope our apples will be all right. We can't know for sure yet."

"*Ach,* the apples! They will bring more than strawberries. I should have thought of them first."

"The orchard's in a warmer spot. We hope for the best. Now fetch me the butter from the cellarway and let us hurry. Father will be in and no meal on the table."

When Father did come it was as though he guessed

Martha's thoughts. For the first thing he said was, "The rain falls on the just and unjust, remember. Life is like that. Better luck will be yours next year, no doubt."

The day after the frost Grandma Sherfey drove over to bring Martha the eight turkey eggs to hatch beneath a broody hen. She said her berries were ruined, too, and she guessed she would put in more beans this year so she could sell some of them to make up for the loss.

"Can I sell off the turkeys in the fall?" Martha asked. "That would help."

Mother nodded. "We'll keep one for Thanksgiving and one for Christmas. The rest you can sell. But you mustn't count your chickens before they hatch. Remember?"

"*Ja*, you are right," Grandma said. "Who knows what can happen? An egg or two may not be good. Or the old hen may turn giddy and let them get cold someday."

So although Martha took heart she tried not to expect eight turkey eggs to become baby turkeys and then all grow up to be fat hens.

"Turkeys are hard to raise," Mother cautioned. "You must watch them carefully. They must not get wet when small. And noise frightens them."

"Give them smearcase, for cottage cheese with onion tops cut up in it is good for them," Grandma advised. "Now here," she said to Mother, "carpet rags I brought for you."

"A rug for the parlor!" Martha exclaimed. "I'll help cut them and sew them together."

"I'll braid them," Mother decided. "To have them woven by the weaver in Dublin would cost such a much."

"A braided rug will do for now," Grandma agreed. "I thought to talk Grandpa into parting with that love seat and rocker, but so angry about the reaper he is, he would not listen."

"Next year with egg money I can buy a few furnishings at a sale. Rockers can be picked up for a quarter at times. I'll start with that."

Martha knew Mother meant an auction sale that would be held when some family sold out to go west or to retire to town because they had grown old. Neighbors would go to the sale and bid for whatever they needed, whether it was garden tools, dishes, furniture, or animals.

"It takes time to get your house together," Grandma said. "And longer if money goes for foolishness."

Martha and Mother exchanged quick glances, knowing Grandma meant not just a reaper, but such things as Mother's black-satin bonnet.

Grandma will be some surprised, Martha thought, when Father allows Mother to make up that pretty piece into a bonnet for me! She carefully avoided looking toward the buffet where it was hidden in a drawer.

Thus the month of April ended, and it was May. During the day Martha studied in school, still dreaming too much, and struggling with the arithmetic problems. At night she helped Mother sew the carpet rags so that by the time folks came to see the reaper work, at least there would be a rug on the parlor floor!

The last day of school Father planned to give out Merit Awards. He sat at the kitchen table while Martha and Mother sewed, and carefully he printed each small certificate. Johnny was reading his geography book. Martha thought the kitchen a cozy place then, with each at work on a project.

"Will I get a certificate?" she asked one evening.

"Not in arithmetic, that is for sure," said Father.

Johnny laughed, and Mother asked, "Is she still the cow's tail, always behind?"

Father nodded, and Martha said, "*Ach*, well, but I'm better than I used to be."

"That is so. But for arithmetic a Merit Award you'll never get once."

Martha put down her sewing to watch Father print a card stating that one of the students of John Sherfey's school in Hilltown Township, Bucks County, that year of 1884, excelled in reading. Father drew a design of wheat sheaves in each corner, with dainty scrolls connecting them, and Martha thought that even when Father was working at such a task he had the reaper in the back of his mind.

I'm good at reading. It would be nice to win that award. I'd keep it always, pressed in my Bible, and the design Father made would always remind me of this first year in our own home when we all worked to earn the reaper.

"The Merit Award cards are like fracturs," Mother

said. "My father had one that he earned in school. In those days they were more elaborate. His teacher painted roses and hearts on it."

"What happened to it?" asked Martha.

"That I don't know. Such things get thrown out. Few folks save them. And yet they are a lot of work."

"There's a fractur on the parlor wall at Freda's," Martha said. "It is a pretty thing to look at."

"I've seen it." Mother bent her head and continued her sewing. "Lucky it is that traveling fractur men no longer come around."

"Why?" Johnny asked.

"If one came to our door I'd be tempted to order a fine one for our parlor! And there isn't even a chair to sit on yet!"

"It is years since a fractur man made the rounds," said Father. "They used to bring their paints and spend the night with you if you ordered one."

"If one comes by, what would you want?" Martha asked.

"A wedding certificate. With pink hearts and roses like my Father's Merit Award."

So, Martha thought, Mother never has stopped dreaming! I-yi-yi-yi!

Finally the last day of school came. They sang songs and each student recited a piece from memory instead of doing real schoolwork. The small boys cut up and Father didn't scold them. Although they would be free of school for the next four months, the boys would work in the fields. The big boys who had stopped weeks ago were here today for the exercises.

> "No more teachers, no more books,
> No more teacher's sassy looks!"

Johnny and Matt chanted those words under their breath and Martha whispered to Sarah,

> "Multiplication is vexatious,
> Division is as bad—
> The rule of three perplexes me
> And fractions drive me mad!"

Sarah shook her head in mock dismay and they both giggled.

But when the Merit Awards were distributed, Martha did receive the one for reading and Father's eyes twinkled when he gave it to her. It was the one with the sheaves of wheat! She tucked it carefully into her apron pocket.

Sarah received the arithmetic award and Johnny had one for geography. He had learned to name all the capitals of the United States and could draw a map putting them in the correct places.

When it was time for dismissal, Father announced that he would not teach next fall, that the school board had hired a woman. Pete Loux and Abe Kratz, both eighteen years old, gave low whistles, and Martha saw Father's lips twitch. A woman teacher would have a time with these boys, she thought.

Father's glad not to teach, but only farm! But what if we don't earn enough to make the last reaper payments?

Her turkeys were hatched now and they were scrawny little things, all neck and a few pin feathers. She must feed them well so they would grow up into fine, big birds.

Bessie had dropped her calf, and Johnny was teaching it to drink milk from a bucket. He put his hand down inside the bucket and let the calf drink by sucking on his fingers. Before long it would be able to drink alone, and by late fall the calf could be sold for veal.

Father is so determined, she thought, that we'll make it. Unless something dreadful happens, like the barn burning down, or a hailstorm ruining the wheat. *Ach,* you have to trust in God and do like Father says, just help yourself yet! Grandpa can't be right all the time!

Linking arms with Sarah, Martha left the schoolhouse. Summer really had started now and in another month the reaper would be delivered to the Sherfeys' farm.

"I-yi-yi-yi." Martha squeezed Sarah's arm. "What a day when our reaper comes!"

9. LIGHTNING STRIKES

JUNE was unusually warm, and Martha picked what strawberries there were and helped Mother make jam. The kitchen was filled with the delicious odor of boiling syrup. There were hotcakes or waffles for breakfast spread with the fresh-made jam.

And every day Martha fed the turkeys as Grandma Sherfey had taught her. One turkey immediately became a family pet, following Martha about the yard and out to the barn. Twice she came into the kitchen and Mother had to shoo her out. Whenever Martha and Mother hung out the clothes, the turkey picked the clothespins from the basket, dropping them on the grass.

"Don't get too fond of her, or you won't want her killed," Father cautioned. "Turkeys are smart fowl and know how to get what they want."

"Remember the turkeys Levi Nace tried to have the men bring from Chalfont up Geil's Hill?" Mother asked.

Father smiled, and Martha and Johnny looked up expectantly. "It was sunset by the time they reached the foot of the hill," he explained, "and those turkeys decided it was bedtime. So every last one of them flew up in the trees and roosted!"

"What did the men do?" Martha asked.

"Nothing they could do. They went home without them. Levi was fit to be tied. He sent them back early next morning and the turkeys flew down as nice as you please and walked right up the hill."

The garden was almost entirely planted now and Martha spent long hours hoeing. Summer was the busiest time of the year and she did not see Sarah except on Sundays at service.

Grandpa Sherfey seldom stopped by—whether because he was angry or too busy, Martha did not know. After service Sundays the discussions and arguments about the reaper went on interminably and always ended the same way. No one really knew if the machine was worth such a large sum. All the men were waiting for the wheat harvest to settle things.

"Come see for yourselves," Father always said. "Delivery's promised in time for the harvest."

Whether or not he was nervous about the outcome, Martha could not tell. She and Mother sometimes talked about it and Mother declared she would be glad when this summer ended.

"Grandpa Sherfey was right about the weather again," Father commented one noon at the table. "He said, 'A wet April and a dry May make a gute crop of hay.' Our hay's about ready. Toward the end of the week it should be just right."

"Are you going to take a load to the Haymarket?" Martha asked. The Haymarket, where Grandpa sold his hay in Philadelphia, was a place that sounded fascinating and Martha often wished she had been a boy so she could go when she was old enough.

"*Nein*. I think we can get along without selling. We'll need a full haymow if we're to feed our four cows and Maud and May clear through to spring. We'll make the reaper payments without hay money, you'll see."

"It is only by all of us working so hard that we manage," Mother said. "As long as nothing goes wrong now —" She hesitated, looking at two flies buzzing near the ceiling. "I think we'll have a storm today. Things are too still. And for every fly I kill another comes to that one's funeral."

Martha shivered. It was all well enough to say things were going well, but she had seen Father poring over his account books, figuring to the last penny how much they had saved and how much they still needed. And ever since she had learned that insurance on barns was forbidden, she was nervous when a storm blew up.

Two Bucks County barns had burned during the first week in June. No fire company could reach a barn in time to save it once the fire started.

Late in the afternoon Mother's prediction came true. The sky darkened and a breeze began to sway the treetops. Father closed the barn door and came to the house. He brought in harness to mend and sat by the kitchen window where the light was better.

Martha was making a shirt for Johnny and thought it was too bad that men and boys did not wear gay colors no matter what their faith. Some men used to wear fancy pants tucked into high stockings and coats with long tails, a white stock at the neck, and frothy cuffs. She had seen pictures of such and the men wore their hair powdered, long and tied back.

The room finally became so dim that Mother lighted a lamp. Johnny played a game with Debbie on the floor and Peter crawled on all fours, jabbering in his own language.

Martha put down her sewing and went to look out the window. Suddenly the rain poured down, drenching the yard. There was a terrific crash of thunder and Debbie put her hands over her ears. After about fifteen minutes the rain stopped as suddenly as it began, but the wind continued to blow and it remained dark. Martha was reminded of the darkness at the tomb of Jesus. How frightening it must have been. The storm now seemed to be going in circles.

A roar of thunder was followed by a streak of lightning that zigzagged across the sky, and as Martha watched it darted toward the barn roof. She caught her breath, staring in unbelief. Father jumped from his chair to stand beside her.

"*Ach*, it's struck the barn," he said, and before Martha took in his words he raced out the door. Over his shoulder he called, "The cows are to pasture. I'll get Maud and May out. Ring the dinner bell!"

Mother ran to the side of the house where the big dinner bell stood on top of a pole. She grabbed the rope and gave it a vigorous pull. The rope, which was an old one put there by the last owners of the house, was frayed at the top and broke off in her hands.

"I-yi-yi-yi," Mother said, "see now. We never used the bell with no hired help in the fields, but we should have tried it."

Martha ran for a broom and tried to reach the brass bell with this, but neither she nor Mother was tall enough.

"Johnny could crawl out on the roof to reach it," Martha suggested.

"Johnny, do that." Mother's voice was almost a sob. She caught up Peter, who had crawled through the doorway. "Martha, you and I must fill buckets."

Martha knew that the dinner bell was to summon Jake Kratz and Joe Godshalk. But she also knew that by the time they arrived it might be too late. Billows of smoke poured through the barn door now, but Maud and May had run safely out to stand whinnying by the pasture gate. There was no sign of Father.

He must be trying to save the pigs. But why doesn't he come out?

Martha caught up a bucket Mother had filled and ran toward the barn. The water slopped over the side and wet her long black stockings and drenched her high black shoes.

What use to run if I spill it all before I get there? she thought impatiently.

Behind her she heard the dinner bell ring, "Bong, bong, bong." So Johnny had reached it from the roof. Martha tripped in one of the deep barnyard ruts and just caught herself in time.

At the door she set the bucket down and called. For a minute there was no reply and her heart pounded. She could see flames rising in the haymow and the sound of their crackling was terrifying. Then she heard Father's voice. It was muffled, but she made out his words.

"Where are you, Martha? I can't find the door for the smoke."

Now Martha knew real terror. The building no longer mattered. Suppose the walls went before Father found his way out? Grandpa told once of a fire where a man was trapped inside and never got out. She looked frantically toward the house for Mother and discovered that Debbie was screaming hysterically and Mother was carrying her back to the house where she already had penned up Peter.

"*Father!*" Suddenly Martha found her voice. "This way!"

With no hesitation she took off her apron and dipped it into the bucket of water. Then she wrapped it around the lower part of her face, covering her nose and mouth.

Dropping on hands and knees, Martha moved slowly through the barn door. It was an eternity before she could make out the cows' stalls and she passed them slowly. Then her eyes stung from the smoke and she closed them to feel her way.

Here was the partition that ran the length of the barn. If she could follow it a little way, she could find Father for he must be near the pigpens at the back. The sound of the fire above her grew louder. Suddenly her head bumped into something hard, and opening her eyes she discovered it was Father and she had knocked against his head. He clutched her firmly and swung her around.

Together they crawled on hands and knees as rapidly as possible back the way she had come. There were several agonizing moments that seemed hours long and then Martha felt the smooth stone of the doorsill and they were outside. Father caught her up and they hurried to Mother, standing white and shaken nearby. The dinner bell was still sounding from the house.

"All right we are," Father said, his voice hoarse. "*Ach*, don't cry. Martha brought me out."

"Why ever did you take such a chance?"

"I couldn't stand hearing those pigs screech after I got Maud and May. But for all my going in I don't think they made it."

"The pigs don't matter so long as you and Martha are safe," Mother said.

Then they heard the gallop of horses and the sound of wagon wheels on the road as Jake and Joe came from each direction. The next ten minutes blurred in Martha's memory ever afterward. The barn was too far gone to be saved, so the men carried as much water as they could and threw it on the chicken-house roof to prevent it from catching fire. Martha pumped and pumped, and when her arm was tired, Mother took her place.

At last with a great roar, the barn timbers gave way and the building collapsed. Huge flames shot toward the sky and then gradually faded away. Jake and Joe, Father, Mother, Johnny, and Martha stood silent at a safe distance watching. Martha saw Mother brush a tear from her cheek. That was all.

"We have much to be thankful for," Father said. "Maud and May are safe, and the cows, too, and this happened before harvest.

"And what I'm most grateful for—Martha brought me out."

Martha suddenly felt as though her knees were going to give way. Father was right. God had been good. Suppose she had not reached Father in time? She must have been guided.

"You won't be able to buy the reaper now, though," she said. "Do you think they will refund your money?"

Father put one arm around her and one around Mother. "We can build a new barn someday by cutting timber in our own woods. And the reaper we must have. It will be my livelihood."

"Say, now," said Joe, wiping his perspiring face with a red handkerchief, "you won't be downed, will you? If you prove this reaper is good—you'll be some smarter than your pop for all!"

"*Nein*," Father answered, "just more stubborn yet." They all managed to laugh at this, even though a bit shakily.

"When you're ready to rebuild," Jake said, "you know the men of the church will give you a hand. Insurance we may forbid, but help you we will!"

"Thanks, Jake. I guess since I have no barn I'll take my first hay to the Haymarket after all."

"And pay more on that reaper? Foolish you are." Joe shook his head. "It's too much money. Why don't you wait a year, anyway? You're just getting started on your own here."

"*Ja*," Jake agreed, "by hand your wife and kids can follow your father's old reaper and bind a couple of acres a day. Who needs to beat that?"

But when they saw that her father would not change his mind, Joe and Jake left. Obviously, they did not believe the Sherfeys would be able to pay for their reaper after this disaster.

Martha stared sadly at the smoking ruin of the barn for a long time. Could Joe and Jake be right, believing like Grandpa?

Suddenly she brightened as she remembered her father had said he would go to the Haymarket. If only she could go! Not only to see the market, but to visit Strawbridge and Clothier's store! *That* would be a day to remember!

10. THE FRACTUR MAN

It was when they were finally eating supper after Father
was sure the fire was out, that Martha asked, "May I
go with you to Haymarket? You'll need someone to give
you a hand and Johnny's not big enough yet."

"I-yi-yi-yi," Mother protested, "a girl cannot go to
Haymarket."

"Why can't I wear boys' clothes? Nobody'd need
know. The city I never have seen and may never get
to see unless I go now."

Father was silent for some time thinking it over.
Martha scarcely dared breathe.

"I would say no," he said at last, "except you acted as
good as any boy today. Would you pass me your promise
that you'd not let on to anyone?"

"*Ach*, I promise!"

"Not even Sarah," Mother said quickly. "Such be-
havior for a girl would cause talk."

"Not even Sarah!"

"It's an eight-hour ride in a hay wagon," Mother

added, frowning. "I don't think you could stand it."

"I could break the journey by staying at the German-town Tavern," Father said. "Then make an early start from there next morning."

"By gum," Johnny said, "you have all the luck."

"You'll get to go another year. You're growing fast."

"Well," Father said, "we'll harvest the hay as soon as it is dry enough."

It was not until she and Mother were doing the dishes that Martha whispered, "Do you think Father will let me see Strawbridge and Clothier's store?"

Mother's tired face lighted momentarily. "Likely he will," she said. "I'm sorry I have no money for you to make a purchase. But looking is nice, too."

Martha thought it was just as well Mother had no cash. If she had, Martha was sure she would be tempted to buy enough pink yardage for a dress. The very thought of the counter loaded with goods made her tingle all over.

The following day Goldie and her eleven pigs turned up in Kratzes' woods. Only the hair on their backs had been scorched and their ears singed. The Sherfeys really rejoiced then. Mother baked a big spongecake and made a pitcher of raspberry shrub to celebrate.

"I'll sell off a couple right away," Father said. "Then the rest I can pen in the field. Martha, one of those I sell will be yours. You tended them."

Martha was immediately worried at the possibility of having her own money. The family would expect her to put it into the reaper fund but if she actually had cash in her hand, how could she stand staring at all the dress goods and not buy?

That very day Father took the pigs to Doylestown and sold them to the slaughterhouse. By afternoon when he returned he said the hay was ready for cutting and they all went to the field. Debbie was put in charge of Peter under a maple tree.

Father drove the mower and Mother, Martha, and Johnny raked the sweet-smelling grass into piles. The next day they would turn it and then Father would start loading a wagon.

It was a long afternoon and while Martha raked she thought about the money Father had pressed into her hand from the sale of a pig. She had taken it to her room reluctantly and placed it in a tiny bag that she hid under her pillow.

There's enough there to buy the gayest material Strawbridge and Clothier's counter can possibly have. What would Mother and Father say if I bought some for myself? And pink, at that!

Remembering Father's advice, Martha went to her bureau drawer and took out the bead ring. She stared at it for a long, long time, slipping it on her finger for a minute. It felt oddly cold.

Then with a sigh she put it away again and undressed for bed. Looking at the ring had not helped. She still wanted a pink dress.

Between the excitement of thinking about the city

trip and the temptation to take the money with her, Martha slept little that night. And she was silent the next morning when she worked again in the hayfield. Constantly in her mind's eye there was a picture of Freda's many pretty clothes.

She tried to concentrate on the reaper and how much it meant to the entire family, but she could not. If she bought the material now, there was time to work on the dress so that it would be ready by the time Mother had the snitz party in the fall. How Sarah would stare.

But so would Grandma Sherfey! And she would do more than stare. She and Grandpa would have plenty to say! And she didn't even have the flowered bonnet yet.

Father loaded the hay wagon with great care.

"It's a tricky job," he explained, as the others forked the hay up to him and he stamped it down evenly, moving slowly around the four sides of the wagon.

"If a load is the least bit tipsy, it will turn over on the way and then I'd have to come home and start all over again."

Martha remembered how particular Grandpa Sherfey was when he loaded his wagon for the Haymarket. No one else was allowed in the wagon. He loaded from the barn, which was considerably easier as the hay would drop down from the mow, instead of having to be forked up from the ground.

Grandpa took so much hay at one time that he used five horses to pull the wagon. Father always had gone with him because he was expert at handling them.

Slowly the wagonload rose higher and higher. Martha's arms ached from the constant tossing. The sun was warm and perspiration poured down her face.

Just as they were almost finished Father watched a horse and buggy jog down the road and turn into their barnyard.

"Johnny and I will finish. You two go to the house," he said to Mother and Martha.

Thankfully Martha went with Mother to pick up Peter and Debbie. When they reached the house, the driver of the buggy was waiting for them by the front porch.

"Gute day," he said. He was a bent little old man with white hair and a pointed beard. Martha tried not to stare and when he smiled at her, she dropped her eyes. Rolled up in his hands were several papers that he began to show Mother.

"Fracturs," he said. "You like? *Taufscheine, Geburtsscheine, und Toten-scheine!*"

Martha knew these words meant baptism, birth, and death certificates. She saw Mother's eyes light with excitement. Mother handed Peter to Martha and took the certificates from his hands. They were hand-printed, and the lovely illuminated lettering made her catch her breath.

"A wedding certificate—do you have a wedding certificate?"

"In the buggy," the man said. "*Ja.*"

Almost as one in a dream Mother followed the old

man to the barnyard. Martha went with them, still carrying Peter and with Debbie shyly holding onto her skirt. Whey they reached the carriage, Mother and Martha stared with interest at the fractur man's equipment. He opened his color box to display its contents.

The wooden box was about a foot long and six inches wide with several compartments for bottles, ink well, etc. Martha examined the fine quill pen, the knife for cutting pen points, the brushes with their different-size tips. The inkwell was blue glass and Martha thought it the prettiest she had ever seen.

But the ruler really caught her eye. One side of it was decorated with rectangles, triangles, running vines of ivy, dainty tulips, and roses. The reverse side showed the letters of the alphabet, drawn in elegant Old English script. At one end was a date, 1769.

"You like my ruler, not so?" he asked. "It was my father's. He always said it belonged to the Mennonite, Christopher Dock."

"I know," Martha said, "the German schoolmaster who taught on the Skippack. He wrote 'One Hundred Rules for Conduct of Children.' Father talks of him."

"*Ja,*" the fractur man said, "Christopher Sauer in Philadelphia printed his book on school management."

"He was the one who rewarded his pupils," Martha recalled. "That's how Father thought to make the Merit Awards."

"*Ja,* it was Dock said when a child learned his ABC's his father was to pay him a penny and his mother fry him two eggs. It was a quaint idea. Then he painted fracturs for Merit Awards. Many of his students learned fractur painting. They did it for years after his death."

"Where do you come from?" Mother asked.

"I am Daniel Kunder," he said. "My wife and I lived at the Ephrata Cloisters and last winter she died. I thought on the road I would go for the summer. Fractur painting I did at the Cloister—songbooks and front pages for Bibles."

Martha knew of the Cloisters at Ephrata, not far from Lancaster. Here men and women who followed the teachings of Conrad Beisel retired from the world to live the religious life.

They were not Mennonites, but belonged to a sect called Dunkers or Seventh-Day Baptists, Father once said. Both men and women wore special nuns' and monks' clothing, living in separate buildings and meeting together for prayer and singing of hymns. During the Revolution, Father said, one of their buildings was used as a hospital and General Washington stayed there.

Martha looked at the old man curiously. He must have abandoned his monk's white robe when he took to the road.

"Here is my notebook," he said. "Perhaps something in it you would like and I make it just for you. A wedding certificate perhaps?"

Mother spoke quickly. "Too expensive they are for me. I have no money. We Mennonites do not buy for fancy."

Martha watched Mother's face. She longed to have a fractur for the parlor, that was certain.

"*Ach*, well," Kunder said, "sometimes I make a trade. But if you want something cheap you can buy a printed birth certificate for your daughter here, and I will letter in the date for ten cents, the place for fifteen cents, and your name and your husband's for twenty-five cents. My prices are not high."

"Couldn't you make a trade and get the wedding certificate you want?" Martha asked. "So nice it would be! The printed ones are not so nice."

"You are right," said Kunder. "But a hand-painted wedding certificate always you could treasure. It would become a family piece, handed down someday from one generation to another."

Peter was stretching out his hands for the contents of Kunder's box and Debbie had lost her shyness and was reaching for the papers in Mother's hands. Mother looked distracted and bit her lower lip nervously.

"Could you make pink hearts on it and maybe an angel at the top?" she asked then.

"*Ja.* If your man is gute he would want you to have such a thing. Fractur men died out long since as you know, and I am the only one on the roads."

"What would you trade for?" Mother asked. "I have eggs, butter, a loaf of fresh-made bread, and doughnuts."

Kunder thought a moment. "Eggs are ten cents a dozen. Make it five dozen and two pounds of butter?

Have you two fat hens? Then throw in a loaf of your bread and a few doughnuts."

Martha knew Mother would hate to part with a laying hen. But it would take Kunder some time to paint the fractur. If she took a printed one, there was little labor involved and he would sell for a small amount of cash.

"Where will you paint it?" Mother still hesitated.

"If you can put me up, I'll do it in your own kitchen this night."

"Tonight we go to bed early. My husband goes to the Haymarket at half after four in the morning."

"Well, no matter. I can do it wherever I stay. Then in the morning I bring it by for you."

Martha waited for Mother's answer, her eyes anxious. Suddenly Martha remembered the money tied in the bag and hidden beneath her pillow.

"You can have my money," she said. "It is upstairs."

Mother smiled. "*Nein*, your money I cannot take. You fed Goldie and cured the pigs of the scours. I could not take it for a fractur. And I shouldn't spend any of our money, either. We need other things first, not so?"

Martha could not answer. She knew it was so, but she hated to admit it.

"Well," Kunder said, "you are a good Mennonite woman. I would like you to have one of my *scheines*, but up to you it is. If you cannot buy, you cannot. That I understand."

He put away his notebook, placed his box on the seat, and climbed into the buggy.

"Gute luck to you," he ended from the buggy seat. In a moment he was off.

"Safe journey," Mother called.

Martha wondered how Mother could stand there so quietly and let this opportunity disappear down the road. She longed to call the old man back.

"Were you afraid of what Father might say?" she asked then.

"*Nein.*" Mother took Peter from Martha and suddenly tossed him in the air to make him laugh. "But my hens, my butter, and eggs must pay my part toward the reaper payments. We all work together, not so? The doughnuts and bread—we eat them tonight and tomorrow for breakfast."

"I would have traded."

Mother did not reply, but began fixing Peter's supper. Martha watched her. She must be tired from haying as I am, she thought. And she remembered the look of longing on Mother's face when she first saw the fracturs.

At supper Mother explained to Father about the fractur man, but he made no comment about her not buying one. He did seem to smile at Mother with his eyes, but no words were exchanged.

When Martha went early to bed so that she could rise in time to go with Father she took out the bag with her money in it. Over and over she counted it. Here was her one chance for a pink dress. At last she made up her mind.

My money I will take to the city. If I see material I like I will buy it. I have wanted such for a long time. Mother let the chance of a lifetime slip. When my turn comes, I will not do so.

She turned over restlessly and slipped her hand beneath the pillow to feel the bag.

Opportunity knocks but once, and this time yet I'll answer the door.

11. ON THE ROAD

MARTHA sat very straight on the high seat of the hay wagon next to Father. She felt odd in Johnny's work pants which Mother had let down for her and in a shirt of Father's which was much too big. She had tucked the shirt inside the pants and wore a pair of suspenders to hold them up.

Beneath the shirt Martha could feel the bag with her money. It hung by a string around her neck and was a constant reminder of her plan. Her plaits were pinned up under an old knitted cap.

Maybe I'm dreaming and I'll wake up in bed. This can't be me driving to Philadelphia!

They had started out as soon as Father finished milking. Just driving through the streets of Doylestown was exciting, although it was so early that the shops were closed and there was no sign of life in the inn yard. Martha stared at the big courthouse building, which Father said had the only circular courtroom in Pennsylvania. He had been to court sessions, but Martha knew she never could attend. Women did not go to such places.

The wagon rolled out of town and along the Norristown Pike. Father talked of the old toll roads and how the stagecoaches used to pass along here, making their way to Allentown, Bethlehem, and Philadelphia. At Chalfont they turned onto Limekiln Pike and climbed the hill outside the town.

Although the distance from home was only seven miles, Martha already felt as though she had gone hundreds of miles. The houses were much like those in Hilltown Township. They were neat white clapboard, or stone, and the barns were painted red with hex signs of moons, stars, and circles done in white. Farmers working in their hayfields or women in their gardens waved as they passed by.

Father encouraged Maud and May when the hill was steep. "Now, girls," he'd say, "take it easy and soon you'll be to the top and going down the other side. We got a job to do and you must do your share. You see it's like this—" On and on he talked, and Martha smiled.

Father's fun, she thought. And I'm lucky to have him and not a sour old man for a father.

Then she felt a prick of conscience. Wasn't she ungrateful to have such a plan to spend her money and not help him?

But change my mind now I will not!

Then Father pointed out the house where the farmer lived who once tied fancy bows on all his cockerels. They were bows his wife saved from candy boxes and just for devilment he put one on the tail feathers of his young roosters.

At another place, after waving a greeting to a very fat woman, he related how one winter she went for a sleigh ride, and when she sat down on the high seat of the sleigh it tipped over backward and she was tossed into the snow.

As the sun rose higher and higher they met more hay wagons and an occasional market wagon that was bound for Conshohocken Market.

"This winter I might go to market." Father studied a farmer's load. "I could rent a stall and sell Mother's butter and eggs—then she won't have to pay the commission men. The apples are doing well and we'll have a big crop to sell. Your turkeys would bring a *gute* price there."

"Johnny and I could pick nuts in our woods," Martha said, thinking that since she intended spending her money today she had better devise other ways of making money.

Her father nodded. "Mother's bread will go well and her shooflies and *fastnachts*."

"Remember when I was *Fastnacht* at Grandpa's?" *Fastnachts*, or doughnuts, were always fried on Shrove Tuesday, or *Fastnacht* Day. The last person downstairs that morning is "the lazy one" and is a cause for ridicule. He is the *Fastnacht*.

"When we butcher," Father continued, "there'd be scrapple, sausage, and head cheese."

Martha began to see that Father was figuring out a way to obtain an income to replace his teacher's salary. Did he worry a great deal about those reaper payments that would cost him 6 per cent interest?

"But I'm afraid it would be too much work for Mother," he ended.

"I can help." I must! But not with my first cash money!

"*Ja*, you do already. But this would mean much more cooking and baking. To have a hired girl would mean less profit even if she only were paid a dollar and a levy a week."

"How much is a levy?"

"Twelve cents."

"In September I'll be thirteen. Enough schooling I've had. Hardly any other Mennonite girls go longer."

"We'll see."

If I leave school to help Mother, then I'll be doing my share. It isn't disobedience to buy dress material with my own earnings. It's not like a gold ring or a cameo pin. And Mother said it is my money to do with as I wish.

Martha tried to picture what her material would be like. It would be some surprise to everyone when she wore her new dress at the snitz party. Such a pretty dress made in the Mennonite fashion would be something different. Even Freda would admire it next winter at Lyceum Meetings at the schoolhouse.

Martha loved Lyceum Meetings. Father always headed one of the debating teams and the men would argue such points as "Which is the greater—anticipation or realization?" The debates became so heated that the audience had many laughs.

And then there was Singing School! I'll take such a big hem that it will last for years even if I grow inches! By the time I'm walking out with someone it will not even be faded if I choose good goods!

A picture of herself riding in a buggy beside a faceless Mennonite boy made Martha stifle a giggle. What would Father think if he could know her thoughts? But suppose no one ever asked her out because folks said she was worldly and wore pink? This was a shattering idea, and Martha quickly pushed it aside.

At noon Father pulled up beside the road and they climbed stiffly down. Mother had given them a lunch of ham sandwiches, potato salad, pickles, and chocolate cake which tasted wonderful as they sat on the grass under the shade of a leafy oak tree. A cardinal darted from branch to branch and Martha thought that God made the birds with bright plumage. Why couldn't people wear fine clothes?

"Tired?" Father asked. "It won't be much longer now."

Martha did not want to admit how weary she was. If she could relax and lean back against the seat, the trip would not be so wearing. But when they went up a steep hill she sometimes walked to help the horses, and when they went down a steep hill it was nerve-racking. Father applied the brakes, but the load of hay was so heavy it looked as if it would shove the wagon into the horses.

On a curve Martha tensely gripped the seat. Father held the reins lightly and the horses slowed from their steady trot to a walk.

Suppose we tip over? If Father has not balanced the load correctly— The loss of a load of hay would be a financial blow. Martha looked behind her apprehensively. Was the wagon swaying more than usual? Her stomach felt queer.

On the way down the Jarrettown Hill a heavily loaded hay wagon in front of them began to sway and its five-horse team to weave about in the road. Father pulled Maud and May to a stop.

"No use getting too close to that!" he said. "He's got fifty-five hundred or six thousand pounds if he has a single one."

Martha watched with horror. A man thrown from a heavily loaded wagon could be killed! The wagon seemed to be picking up speed and was swaying crazily. They could hear the hoarse shouts of the driver as he tried to stop his horses.

Suddenly the wagon turned over on its side, spilling hay in every direction. The driver was thrown into the ditch and Martha momentarily closed her eyes. Father tossed Martha the reins and jumped down. Before he reached the farmer, the man stood up.

"Jumping Jehoshaphat!" he screamed at his horses. "You numskulls!" He stamped his feet in a frenzy while the horses reared in their traces, trying to free themselves of the overturned wagon.

Father ran to quiet the horses and held their harness until they were calm. Martha talked to Maud and May in an effort to keep them from becoming frightened, and wished Father would hurry back. Suppose Maud and May decided to run down the hill? They would land in the ditch in trying to pass the other team.

The farmer's hay was scattering to the four winds and Martha remembered Father saying that when such a catastrophe occurred a farmer must return home and get a new load. It was no wonder he was so upset.

"He was an addlepated one," Father said later. It had taken a very long time to clear the road so they could pass.

Other teams with wagons had drawn up behind them. Father pointed out the tavern at the bottom of the hill.

"That's the Jarrettown tavern," he said, "and we might as well stop there now that it is so late. We have lost much time and I know you are weary."

Jarrettown had little more than the inn, a general store, and a few houses, Martha saw as they approached. But here was the first test of whether people would recognize her as a girl in boys' clothing. Her heart began to hammer furiously.

The inn's yard was filled with wagons and the tavern keeper stood in the doorway yelling directions at the hostlers.

"*Ach*, John," he called, recognizing Father, "you're late. Not a room left. You'll have to curl up on a blanket on the floor. This your boy?"

Martha felt her face crimson, but Father answered casually, "*Gute* day to you. An accident down the road a piece there was and more wagons are on behind. What's for supper?"

"Sauerbraten, gingerbread, and custard pies," the man replied.

Martha nervously pulled her knit cap down farther over her ears and hoped he would not wonder why in pleasant weather she wore such a thing. There was no woman in sight, although Father said the tavern keeper's wife cooked for the men.

Martha helped Father tend the horses, as he trusted no one to care for Maud and May. They wiped them off thoroughly and gave them a bag of oats and as usual one waited for the other before they began to munch. Martha lugged their water from the pump in the yard, keeping her head ducked low when she passed anyone.

When they entered the inn, the main room was crowded with men who were gathering to eat at a long table. The tempting smell of the pot roast cooked with bay leaves, onions, and gingersnaps made Martha realize how hungry she was, but she was nervous about sitting near so many strangers who thought she was a boy.

Father heaped her plate and his, and they ate silently while the others talked mostly of the price of hay.

"The horsecars make us a gute market," a lanky farmer said with satisfaction as he shoveled in his food.

"*Ja*, there are thousands of horses in the city," said another, "what with everyone who can afford a carriage having at least one horse in his stable."

"They're getting more careful with the weighing," a fat farmer informed them. "Too many farmers trying tricks—they stand on the load to make it weigh heavier. Some use lumber at the bottom."

"I heard there are sixteen hundred head of horses at the car barn at Twentieth and Wharton," the lanky one said.

"There were twenty wagons lined up waiting when I got there last time. It pays to leave early."

"What do you know of this new all-metal reaper?" someone asked then, and Martha resisted poking Father in the ribs.

"McCormick wants too much money for it. He's all the time bringing out a better one every year. My old wire binder will do me yet."

"It's a wonder to me you bought a binder at all. What's the matter, don't your old woman bind fast enough to suit you?"

There was laughter at the man's expense, but he was unruffled. "She can follow after a reaper and keep up better than most men," he bragged. "She can do two acres any day."

"You Mennonite men get the most work out of a woman, I'll say that for you," another man taunted, and Martha lowered her eyes hastily. Didn't other women work as hard?

"That twine binder's too expensive to keep up," the man next to Father said. "Who can pay for all that twine? As long as I farm I'll tie my sheaves with a couple of twists of the grain."

Martha looked quickly at Father and he winked at her. He did not enter into the argument or talk. Martha guessed he had argued enough about the reaper at service on Sundays. He believed in it and that was sufficient for him.

The lanky farmer brought out a zither and placed it on a table. Martha stared, fascinated. She had never seen this musical instrument before, and when the man began to bow the zither with free sweeps of his arm she loved the rollicking melody he brought forth. She hardly tasted her hot gingerbread, smeared with melting butter.

The zither was not quite a yard long and was broader at one end than the other. It was beautifully decorated and had five strings and three bridges.

"Some Mennonite churches," Father said to her, "have zithers for accompanying hymns. Grandpa would not approve, but it is some pretty, not so?"

"Sing something, Jed," the tavern keeper said.

" 'The Monkey's Wedding,' " somebody called out.

" 'Turkey in the Straw,' " said another.

The man obligingly played both, and the men tapped their feet. Some leaned back with lighted cigars or pipes. At last they began to stretch and yawn and as each man wanted to make an early start in the morning, either for the city, or for home, they climbed the staircase to bed.

Martha and her father wrapped themselves in blankets and lay down in the main room by the fire. It had been warm when they first entered, but now the night air was cool. Martha was certain she would have difficulty dropping off to sleep since she had so much to think about. If only she dared tell Sarah about her trip!

She felt again inside her shirt for the bag with the money. It was safe, and by this time tomorrow she would have the dress material!

12. SPRIGGED DIMITY

It was still dark when Father wakened Martha and she stiffly unwrapped herself from the blanket to follow him out of the inn. They were the first up and the inn yard looked eerie with a slight veil of mist rising from the creek nearby.

While Martha waited and Father harnessed Maud and May to the wagon the farmer who owned the zither came out, yawning. He had been to the city the day before and his first act now was to check his wagon, which he had loaded with such provisions as sugar, salt, and other groceries, as well as gifts for his family.

Suddenly he started to swear, yelling for the innkeeper, who soon stuck his head out of a second-floor window.

"My hay money! My hay money's gone yet! I've been robbed!" He danced up and down, cursing the innkeeper.

"Are you sure?" Father hurried to help him search.

"It was all in silver dollars," the man groaned now, "and it was too heavy to carry. So I hid it under the sack of sugar. Somebody found it all right—it's gone."

"You fool!" the innkeeper called down. "Don't you know there are robbers on the roads at night? They have easy pickings from such addlepated ones as you. Lucky you are they didn't take the provisions along with the silver dollars!"

When they finally were on their way, leaving the man angrily harnessing his horses and declaring he never would stop at Jarrettown again, Father said, "Tonight we will have to drive all the way from the city. It will mean a long trip, but you can lie in the back of the wagon and sleep. I won't take any chances on losing my hay money."

The sun was beginning to rise by the time they reached the outskirts of the city and started down Germantown Road. Martha looked with interest at the cobbled street, the houses, and shops. Father pointed out places of interest to her and she felt he was giving her a history lesson, but she did not mind. It was more fun than reading about the places in a book.

There was the Dunker Church where Christopher Sauer, Jr., was a bishop, and Martha was reminded of the fractur man. And when they came to the Mennonite Church, Martha was glad Father stopped Maud and May to let her get a good look at the stone building. Next to it was a small graveyard where early-day families lay buried.

"Here Uncle Horace's family attend meeting," Father said. "William Rittenhouse was the first minister, but the old log meetinghouse was not built until after his death. He had no bishop to baptize or give communion to his people, but he did the best he could for them. Over on the creek he built a paper mill and his house and the mill still stand."

The wagon moved on.

"This was all Pastorius land," Father continued. "Daniel Pastorius and his wife, Sarah, ran the Green Tree Inn during Revolutionary times."

Martha tried to imagine what it had been like in those days, but even the Civil War seemed long ago. Mennonites had not gone to the Civil War, paying for substitutes instead.

People were beginning to appear on the streets now, and Martha wondered if they liked living so close to others. It would be odd to have so many persons living nearby, she thought.

Most interesting to Martha was the building where Christopher Sauer had his first printery, publishing the first German Bible in America in 1743, at the request of the Mennonites.

"He printed the books of Christopher Dock," Martha said, with the fractur man in mind again.

Last of all was the Thones Kunder place where the first protest of the Germans of Germantown against slavery was made in 1688. Perhaps the fractur man was a descendant of Thones!

The streets grew narrower as the wagon worked its way closer and closer to the center of the city. The Haymarket was at Sixth and Callowhill and Martha began to think they would never reach it. But the knowledge that she was getting nearer all the time to Strawbridge and Clothier's store made shivers of excitement go through her.

Then as the wagon rounded a corner, it sideswiped a gas lamppost. Before Martha realized what had happened a crowd gathered and a policeman was bawling Father out.

"You dumb Dutchman!" he shook his head, his hands on his hips. "You and your hay wagons. Always in somebody's way! And they can't get around you!"

"Is it my fault your streets so narrow are?" Father asked mildly.

"So it's the fault of the streets! Well, I fine you ten dollars right now. That'll teach you to watch your horses."

Martha gasped. A boy in the crowd jeered at the policeman and another one jeered at Father. There were catcalls from several rough-looking men.

Martha was glad no one guessed she was a girl, sitting high up on the hay wagon. She put her hands in her pockets and squeezed them into fists to keep them from trembling.

Ten dollars! There would be little profit left when they reached home if Father paid such a sum. Martha looked to see how he was taking this misfortune. He was staring at the policeman now and finally, shaking his head, he reached in his pocket to pull out his worn black purse. After a moment he handed a paper ten-dollar bill to the policeman. Martha knew it must be part of the money put aside for the reaper. Paper bills were rare.

Tears welled in her eyes, and if she had not feared someone would notice, they would have spilled down her cheeks. But suddenly Father handed her the reins and jumped from the wagon.

The policeman watched incredulously as Father took down his log chain and went around to hitch it to the lamppost.

"What do you think you're doing?"

"I always take home what I pay for," Father said.

The policeman sputtered, and then as the crowd roared with laughter he handed Father back his ten dollars. Without a word Father unhitched the log chain and climbed back on the wagon seat.

"Giddap, Maud. Hup there, May," he said, and as the crowd cheered, the hay wagon moved on down the street, the other wagons that had been blocked behind them following. Martha grinned sideways at Father, who winked at her slowly and then gave his full attention to the horses and the cobbled paving.

At last the huge, shed-like building came into sight and Father paused to speak to a man leaning against a building.

"Want a job?"

"Unloading hay?"

Father nodded, and the man followed them into the big doorway where Father drove onto the scales. They were early enough so that they did not have to wait long, and almost at once a buyer stepped up to examine the load.

"Not too many weeds in this one," the man said critically. "Would you deliver it in Germantown instead of unloading here?"

"I don't much want to drive back through those narrow streets," Father said. "Had a little trouble coming in."

"I'll pay you for the trouble," the buyer said. "I've got a livery stable and there'll be somebody to help you unload there."

After some discussion Father turned to the man he had hired outside. "Here's something for coffee and doughnuts," he told him, "guess we'll drive this back."

"Suits me," the man said, leaving them.

"Won't we get to Strawbridge and Clothier's?" Martha barely managed to ask. To be this close and not go to the shop or the downtown streets—and worst of all not to be able to buy her material, after all! The plan she had made had slipped her mind only during the excitement of the policeman. Now, as she realized that she might never reach the store, she felt her hopes dashed.

"Your boy wants to see the sights?" the liverystable man smiled. "Don't blame him. If you want to take a horsecar downtown for an hour or so, I'll keep an eye on the horses and wagon. Then when you come back I'll have bought all I need and can follow you out."

Father's eyes twinkled. "*Ja*, this young one doesn't want to miss anything."

"Aren't you hot with that cap on?" the man asked.

Martha shook her head and prayed Father would do

something to call the man's attention away from her. What would she do if one of her plaits slipped from underneath the cap? She was hot enough right now with her cheeks scarlet from embarrassment.

Soon they were on the horsecar and Martha decided she preferred their own carriage. She was crowded in with so many people and she was afraid every minute that someone would discover she was a girl.

When they reached the store at Second and Market, Martha stared at its size. Never had she seen such a big place. Father said he had shopping of his own to do and left her at the dress-material counter. It was just as Mother had described it—calico, silk, satin, alpaca, dimity, lawn—Martha looked and looked.

The lovely pinks attracted her immediately. This was what she wanted. But which shade? A pale pink, a dusty rose, a pinkish lavender, a deep crimson? Martha reached out to stroke a bolt of the satin, which shimmered richly and took her breath away.

"No touching, sonny," the salesman's voice stopped her with her hand in midair. Suddenly she saw that her hands were none too clean and she swallowed several times before she found her voice to inquire the prices.

"Something for your mother?" the man asked.

Was he looking at her curiously? Did he see that underneath these clothes was a girl and not a boy? Martha's heart beat rapidly. She managed to nod her head.

"What does she want? Something for an afternoon frock?" Then, as though taking in her appearance, "Or a piece of calico for every day? We have some nice serviceable pieces. Here's a dark blue, and a brown that won't show dirt."

Martha shook her head. "No, something pink."

"Pink? You got the money?"

Martha turned her back to him and managed to reach inside her shirt and extract a handful of quarters and a silver dollar from the bag. She held them out for the man to see.

"Fine, fine," the man said. "Now I don't suppose you know how many yards she needs? Did she write a note?"

"Four yards," Martha said firmly. She knew well

enough how much it took for a dress for herself. "But I want to look awhile before I decide."

"Four yards will be skimpy unless she's a small woman," he commented.

Martha's face grew red, but she ignored this. *Ach,* but I hope he waits on somebody else while I decide. To have him staring at me makes me some nervous!

Then her glance fell on a bolt of white dimity sprigged with dainty rosebuds. Wouldn't that be a heavenly piece to make up and match with her bonnet remnant? What would Sarah say when she saw her at service in such an outfit?

But what, too, would Grandpa and Grandma Sherfey say? I don't care! I'll never have such a chance again!

She looked around the store at the busy salespeople hurrying back and forth, the women shopping with their baskets on their arms, and here and there a man dressed most elegantly. There was even one lady nearby who had a bustle! Martha's eyes widened.

Finally she looked back at the sprigged dimity. Even made in Mennonite fashion it would be a dress to catch the eye.

"Four yards of this one," she said at last, but her voice now was only a little above a whisper.

The salesman brought out a pair of shears and laid them on the counter. Then he began to measure off the material, pulling out a yard length at a time and measuring it from his nose to the end of his outstretched fingers. One. Two. Three. Four. He reached for his shears.

Suddenly Martha had a clear picture of Mother's face when she told the fractur man she could not buy a wedding certificate. There had been tears in her eyes, but she held them back and her voice had been firm. But, oh, how Mother had wanted that fractur.

Shame struck Martha like a physical blow.

"Wait! Don't cut it for all! *Ach*, I can't buy it once."

Looking up, Martha saw Father standing waiting for her. How long had he been there?

Without a word Martha joined him and together they walked from the store. But first she handed him the money she was still clutching in her hand. He silently put it in his own purse.

On the street Martha did not see the people they passed, or the shopwindows. She moved along beside Father silently.

It was not until they were seated on the horsecar, with the two horses trotting smartly along and a breeze fanning the air, that Father spoke.

"What made you change your mind?" he asked in a low voice. "I would not have stopped you. It was your money to spend as you pleased."

"It was because Mother didn't buy the fractur," she said. "I-yi-yi-yi, but I never will like dressing plain." The memory of the sprigged dimity was a searing pain.

"Never is a long time," Father said, his eyes smiling at her.

13. THE REAPER
DEMONSTRATION

A WEEK after Martha and Father returned from Philadelphia, the reaper was delivered to the freight station at Doylestown. Father took Johnny with him this time and Johnny told Martha he was sure it was as exciting a trip as her ride to Philadelphia. This made Martha smile. Johnny would never know what it was like to be a girl in boys' clothing, or how she felt at the dress-material counter.

"At every farm women came out on the porch or hung out the window. Men came out on the road to make Father stop so they could take a look. By gum, there will be a crowd the day we harvest!"

Mother began to worry about how many pies she would have to bake, how many extra loaves of bread, whether one ham would be big enough, how many chickens she should cook to make into salad.

"Sarah's mother likely will bring potato salad, rolls, angel cake, and macaroni and cheese," Martha said.

"And Grandma Sherfey will bring the lemon meringue pies, a big pot of baked beans, and chocolate cake." Mother looked about the kitchen distractedly. "So much there is to do yet. Windows must be washed again and fresh curtains hung in the dining room."

All the geraniums from the windowboxes had been planted in a flowerbed in front of the house, so the window sills looked empty. The rag rugs were washed, and they kept shooing Shep off them. Mother had a new tablecloth saved for the table.

On the living-room floor the carpet was laid, made with the carpet rags Grandma had brought. She had complimented Mother on its neatness. It lay flat and smooth, waiting for furniture to be placed upon it. Meanwhile a blue-and-white star quilt that Mother had pieced was stretched onto a frame in there for the women to work on.

"It's the reaper folks are coming to see, not how you housecleaned," Father said. Martha and Mother looked at each other and smiled at such ignorance. The women might look briefly at the reaper, but the house was the important thing to them.

"Granny Godshalk never goes into anybody's kitchen that she doesn't run her finger along the mantel shelf to see if there's any dust," Mother said.

"And Mrs. Kratz always has her clothes on the line earlier on a Monday morning than anybody else," Martha added. "We have two such spick-and-span housekeepers for neighbors yet."

So things went along from day to day, with each one

seeming to grow busier than the day before. And every morning Father took the cover off the reaper to look it over as though he had not seen it before. His excitement was steadily mounting.

If the machine worked as well as Father hoped, Martha knew he counted on farmers hiring him at once. But if they didn't consider it worth while, they would bind their own sheaves by hand and he would have a hard struggle meeting his last payments.

In the wheat field Father studied the heads of grain so often that Mother told Martha she hoped it did not turn out like cooking—"Watch pot, never boil," and the wheat never ripen.

But at last the wheat was ready and word was passed out at Sunday service that on Tuesday Father would demonstrate the reaper. Twelve families planned on coming, and Mother frantically tried to remember which women promised to bring what food. Martha and Sarah were looking forward to being together for an entire day, and Martha wondered if she could keep from telling Sarah about her trip to the city.

Grandpa quoted so many Pennsylvania Dutch proverbs that pointed out the sins of extravagance and the rewards gained from honest labor that there were smiles among the men and women.

"Don't hurry, work steadily," Grandpa said with a shake of his head. "Idleness is the devil's resting place."

Another time it was, "Work faithfully; laziness is worse than a pestilence." And with a wag of his finger he boomed forth, "Earning and saving together produce the surest wealth."

"That's what we are doing," Martha whispered to Mother, who was too upset to do more than nod her head in agreement.

Grandma Sherfey said she did not know whether Tuesday was a gute day or not and she would consult the almanac and see what was forecast for that date. She advised Father to watch his step wherever he went and if he saw a pin to pick it up to bring him good luck.

"I have an idea," Father said when they were driving home from meeting the Sunday before the harvest. "Grandpa has a new argument trying to prove the reaper no good. For some time he has been saying it isn't a strong enough machine, so I told him they had a field test over in Montgomery County. They chained two reapers together, back to back, and then pulled them apart to see which was the stronger. The McCormick was the better by far. The other was too light weight. So now what? Grandpa says it is too heavy a machine and will ruin Maud and May!"

"What are you going to do?" Martha asked.

"Hitch myself in place of the horses to show him its light draft."

"I-yi-yi-yi!" Mother exclaimed. "Injure yourself, you might!"

Father shook his head. "I have tried it. It isn't hard to do."

Mother looked more worried than ever, but they all knew Father was determined.

The morning of the reaper demonstration finally arrived, and Martha was up at five when she first heard Mother stirring. Johnny came downstairs sleepily rubbing his eyes and yawning. Debbie and Peter slept late.

Breakfast was over by six-thirty and all the chores done. Horses and buggies began arriving by seven. Johnny was sent to stand by the white picket fence to tie the animals.

Martha smoothed her hair by the mirror in the kitchen. She wore the brown dress she had made for the Foot Washing Service, and she didn't think of the sprigged dimity too often. She was too busy.

She did not feel virtuous about this, however, because she knew she had been weak to have thought of spending that money on herself at all. She knew her one chance was gone and although she was reconciled to this fact, she was not happy about it. Therefore it was better to put such thoughts out of her mind.

Granny and Joe Godshalk arrived first and Granny said, "Say, now did you know Nate Hunsberger's wife had twins? They want me to come stay awhile, but I said not till after I was here today once! This I wasn't going to miss!"

Jake Kratz walked over with his family, his wife carrying a large kettle of lemonade and each of the children holding some kind of baked goods carefully covered with white napkins. Bishop Rosenberger and his wife were among the early arrivals, too, and Martha saw this made Mother more nervous than ever.

Sarah's family were late, and Martha was relieved when their matched grays trotted up the road. The kitchen soon became crowded. The men went at once to stand talking by the blackened ruin of the barn where Father had hitched Maud and May to the reaper. They examined the machine carefully.

The women inspected the house, admiring the parlor carpet, the blue-star quilt, the pink begonias on the front porch. Mother glowed under their praise.

Grandpa and Grandma Sherfey were among the last to drive up. He looked like a thundercloud and made biting remarks, which Martha overheard when she and Sarah slipped outside. Sarah said right away she was more interested in seeing Martha's turkeys than the reaper, and Martha was glad to get away from the sound of Grandpa's voice.

"Mother says I can raise guineas next summer," Sarah said. "Do you think they're hard to care for?"

"No harder than turkeys. Mother doesn't like the noise guineas make all the time, but the meat is good eating."

"Peacocks would be nice, but you can't eat them." Sarah picked a handful of daisies as they stood watching the turkeys. Martha had brought a pan of corn and she scattered it so that each turkey would get some. They strutted about the pen stretching their necks and rumbling in their throats.

"Back in Bible times people ate peacock tongues. Imagine! Grandma Sherfey says when you hear a peacock scream it means bad luck."

This was the first time the girls had been alone since school stopped and Martha longed to tell about her Philadelphia adventure. She had known it would be this way when she saw Sarah. They always shared things.

Ach, well. Perhaps someday when we're grown up and married, with daughters of our own, then I can tell of the time I was in Strawbridge and Clothier's and came so close to buying four yards of dimity sprigged with roses for a dress.

Then the girls saw the men head for the wheat field. Maud and May were pulling the reaper and Father sat very straight on the seat. Johnny was on Maud's back.

"Let's run," Martha said, her heart pounding. She saw the women hurry from the house and the children raced up and down screaming at each other.

"It's like a big picnic," Sarah commented.

"Only at this picnic it matters what happens," Martha said. She did not think Sarah realized how important this reaper test was to the Sherfeys. Father would be laughed at for years to come if the machine was not a success today.

When the girls reached the field, the men and women were lined up along the fence. Martha joined Mother and the two exchanged quick glances.

Father drove the team to a corner of the field and when he began to use the reaper there was dead silence. Even the children hushed their noise. Suddenly Martha thought the sun seemed unusually bright. She could scarcely see the reaper approaching the roadside end of the field.

Gradually her eyes cleared and she saw the machine methodically cut the grain. As the mower cut the stalks off, the binder attachment, which was like a set of giant arms, gathered a number of them together into a bundle, and the ball of twine beside Father's seat bound them quickly together into a neat sheaf.

There were loud cheers from the men and exclamations of amazement from the women. Sam Moyer, Joe Godshalk, and Jake Kratz slipped through the fence and began picking up the sheaves. They stacked a dozen or more together to make tall shocks, talking excitedly as they did so.

Grandpa Sherfey stood silently staring at the reaper and the ever-lengthening row of cut grain. Martha wondered if he might be thinking of his early life when he cut all the wheat on his father's farm with a scythe. She thought the field before them looked just like the reaper advertisement that Father had shown them last spring.

Was Grandpa going to admit now that Father had made a wise investment?

Father unhitched Maud and May after he rounded the field and was ready to make the square again. He stepped in front of the shaft, and, bending, picked it up. Calling Johnny to sit on the seat, Father pulled the reaper partway down the field to prove that it was not too heavy a machine for the horses.

Grandpa still did not speak, but at last he stooped to

slip through the fence rails. He joined the men shocking up the wheat. His face was stern, however, and Martha knew that he was not ready to give in.

The women finally returned to the house to quilt and enjoy themselves talking. Martha and Sarah tended the small children, talking all the while. When noontime came, the women carried the food out under the maple trees in front of the house and everyone sat on the grass with checked tablecloths spread out before them. Plates heaped with food kept the cloths from blowing in the breeze.

Martha was pouring a second cup of coffee for

Grandpa when he said to her, "*Ach*, well, Martha, you can afford to be a Fastnacht any time you want now, not just on Fastnacht Day. Your father will have time on his hands with such a machine to do his work."

"It works so easy maybe I'll let Martha drive the team," Father joked. "Then I can be the Fastnacht, not so?"

Martha saw Grandpa was in no joking mood. "You'll need to hire out many a day if you're ever to pay for that contraption," he declared. "All that interest they're charging you will leave you with empty pockets."

"I'm going to stand market at Conshohocken," Father said.

"You'll need to have such a much to sell," Grandpa said. "Who can afford all that twine for such a binder? Two long pieces of grain looped together is good enough for me, but that has to be done by hand!"

"We've got a gute crop of apples coming," said Father.

"Apples!" Grandpa snorted. "Apples alone will not be enough."

"Why can't we make apple butter?" Martha spoke up before she remembered she should be seen and not heard. "Home-made apple butter city folks might like. Mother and I could make it the day after the snitz party."

"Snitz party?" asked Sarah.

Everyone smiled as Mother said this was a good time to invite them all to the snitz party they planned as soon as the apples were ripe.

"Pick a gute day," Grandma Sherfey cautioned, "or your apple butter won't keep!"

"We'll have it on the twenty-first of October—that is Martha's birthday," said Mother.

"You'll need more than a lucky day," Grandpa interrupted. "Anyone who spends money like he was born with a silver spoon in his mouth needs plenty of luck. Here are twelve men loafing when they should be home cutting and binding their own wheat by hand! Me, I'm going home to work!"

With that Grandpa stood up and headed for his horse and buggy.

"Never mind Grandpa," Grandma whispered to Mother, embarrassed. She hurried off after him.

Everyone talked then and Martha decided they still thought Grandpa might be right. But despite this Jake, Joe, and Sam told Father they wanted him to harvest for them. That made them all smile.

When everyone had departed, Father said, "We're going to weather through no matter what Grandpa thinks. It's like we said—all of us working together can do the impossible. We'll pick apples in September, have that snitz party, and you women can make the apple butter like Martha suggested. Not so?"

Ach, Father calls me a woman now. I won't be doing problems on a blackboard this winter. I'd better start that dower chest like Sarah, for sure!

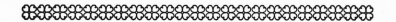

14. THE SNITZ PARTY

THE summer went by in a rush of work. Father was gone much of the time, harvesting with his reaper, and Johnny went with him.

Martha and Mother tended the garden, made sauerkraut, corn relish, chowchow, dill pickles, sweet pickles, sour pickles, and bread-and-butter pickles. They dried corn, dried beans, dried peas. There was always the delicious smell of spices in the kitchen, and long pans of drying vegetables soaked up the sun on the back porch.

In September they dug potatoes, pulled beets and carrots to store down cellar. Then Father pronounced the apples ripe, and each day they spent hours in the orchard. There were Winesaps, Smokehouse, Smith's Cider, and tiny crabapples, which Mother made into amber jelly.

Barrel after barrel was filled, and Martha began to count the days till the twenty-first. Would Grandpa and Grandma come to the snitz party?

No one knew. Not even Grandma. Grandpa had not

come to the house once since the day of the reaper demonstration. After service on Sundays he did not linger
to talk.

"He had a heat stroke in the haymow one day in
August," Grandma whispered to Mother once. "He was
that red in the face he couldn't speak yet. I put him to
bed and sponged him with cool water and he went to
sleep for three hours!"

"Imagine Grandpa in bed in the daytime! Binding all
that wheat with only Abe to help was too much for him
this summer. He knows it, but won't admit it. Maybe
next year he hires John with his binder, not so?" Mother
suggested.

But Martha knew Father did not think so. "He's still
saying that folks pay me too much for the job I do for
them," Father explained.

"Maybe if you did his for less?" Martha asked. She
wished every day that Grandpa would "get over his mad."

Sometimes it seemed that all the family could talk
about was Grandpa. And that the whole neighborhood
was talking also.

One day each week Father carried as much baked
goods and vegetables as Mother could spare to Conshohocken Market. Johnny went here also, but Martha
did not mind. She was satisfied now that she had seen
the city. Her visit to Strawbridge and Clothier's store
seemed like a dream of long ago.

"I must get to the woods one of these days and start
cutting," said Father one day. "It will take a lot of

lumber for the new barn. It must be built before winter sets in."

There was so much to be done there were not enough hours in the day to do it all. It was lucky the school had hired a woman to teach, for Father was far too busy. He had lost weight and every night he worked at his accounts.

"Mother won't have parlor furnishings for another year, but we'll make that last reaper payment by December," he repeated continually.

If only Grandpa had not been angry, they would be happy. But no one liked having bad feelings like this in the family.

Mornings were cooler now, but the afternoons were bright with sunshine. When the apple trees were bare of fruit, Mother made preparations for the party.

"What will happen if Grandpa doesn't come?" Johnny asked Martha. "Won't he ever come visiting any more, or we go there?"

"I wish I knew," Martha answered. She tried to think of her birthday and forget Grandpa, but that was impossible.

Finally the day came. It was even more of a mad rush than the day of the reaper demonstration. Martha's birthday cake was saved for the party in the evening, and she and Mother baked shoofly, apple, and pumpkin pies.

Chairs and benches were brought from Kratzes' and Godshalks' and crowded into the kitchen. The room was spotlessly clean and Martha thought of how it would look tomorrow, with apple juice spattered here and there. The cleaning would all have to be done over again. But that was the life of a housewife, she acknowledged.

Debbie was allowed to stay up, but Peter was put to bed before anyone arrived. Father moved the last barrels of apples from the cellar and suddenly folks started arriving.

Moyers were first this time, to Martha's delight, and Sarah gave her a beautifully hemstitched bolster case.

"To start your dower chest," Sarah said, her eyes twinkling.

Both girls laughed then. Neither of them was returning to school. Johnny and Matt would bring them tales of the new teacher and they would get to know her only when she came to board at their homes.

As the women poured into the kitchen they put on work aprons over their immaculate white ones and set to work. The men, too, were swathed in aprons and no time was wasted. Even boys such as Johnny and Matt did their share.

Tongues wagged as fast as fingers worked, Martha noticed. Neighborhood gossip was relayed from one woman to another, and as each new family arrived the Sherfeys hoped it might be Grandpa and Grandma. No one mentioned their absence, but everyone took note of it. It gave Martha a jumpy feeling.

Gradually the dishpans began to fill with apple parings and the thin apple slices were spread out on long pans. Tomorrow Martha and Mother would tend the huge copper boiler outside over an open fire. Quarts and quarts of apple butter would fill Mother's jars for Father to take to market. Strings of snitz for winter pies would soon hang in the attic.

But the feeling of well-being this should have brought did not come over Martha. Mother's eyes were shadowed, and Father seemed to be listening for another set of buggy wheels rather than to Joe Godshalk's story.

"Say," Joe said, "did you hear about Levi Nace's new horse? She won't stop for nothing when she thinks it's time to head for home. Levi was to Doylestown the other day and had one of his new hired men along. Before the man could get into the carriage the horse took off and there was no stopping her."

"What did Levi do?" asked Sam Moyer.

"Drove that fool horse clear around town and then managed to get her back by the store where his man waited. Couldn't stop and he had to jump for the buggy while it was rolling by. They say he like to have never made it."

Martha wet her lips nervously. Her mouth was dry. She saw Mother attempt to smile at Joe's story. Then, suddenly, there was the sound of another carriage and Martha flew to the door. Her heart hammered against her ribs when she saw Grandpa and Grandma approach the back porch. They seemed to be carrying something.

She held the door wide for them to enter. Grandpa was holding one end of Grandma's second-best love seat, and she was holding the other. There was a general gasp of surprise from everyone in the kitchen, and Martha saw tears spring to Mother's eyes.

Grandpa and Grandma put the settee down in the center of the kitchen. There was barely room for it, what with the apple barrels, people, chairs, and benches. Grandpa plunked himself down on the love seat and stretched out his long legs.

"*Ach,*" he said, "she wouldn't leave me be till we brought this thing. But every man has to earn his own salt, I say. So if you want this settee you can cut my grain next summer with that newfangled reaper you're so daffy about."

For a moment Martha thought Father would refuse the offer. She knew Grandpa had made too stiff a bargain. Then she saw Father and Mother exchange quick looks and Father's eyes twinkled.

"Your wheat I'll harvest, but your oats you can pay me to cut, not so?" Father went back to paring the apple he held in his hand as though Grandpa's answer did not matter. The room was very still and Martha did not breathe.

"You get too much," said Grandpa, "but I'll have to pay it yet. I'm not so young as I used to be or I wouldn't be making such a bargain. If you'd stayed with me I wouldn't have to use machinery yet. And you're too stubborn to admit the thing cost more than you can afford. You think this apple crop's going to make your last payment for you?"

"My turkeys will help," Martha said before she thought.

Grandpa glared, but before he had a chance to explode Grandma said, "I-yi-yi-yi, I don't want to hear any more reaper talk. That's all I've heard all summer. We came to pare apples. Get off that settee and carry it to the parlor."

Father put down his knife and Grandpa stood up. The two picked up the love seat and left the room. Everyone started talking very loudly and Mother caught Martha's hand and pulled her toward the parlor. They stood in the doorway to see how fine the room looked with the love seat standing on the rag carpet.

"It's nice even without a fractur on the wall," Martha said, and Mother smiled in agreement.

When they returned to the kitchen, Sam Moyer was speaking. "How about all of us coming next week to build John's new barn? Think you can have a load of lumber ready by then?"

Father nodded, and Grandpa said, "I'll bring Abe over tomorrow to give you a hand. Think you can feed two extra men while you make apple butter?"

Mother nodded this time. Talk rose and fell about the room. Granny Godshalk said when she was taking care of Amelia Appenzeller she found Amelia only washed her rag rugs every other week. Sarah and Martha smiled at Granny's satisfaction.

Sarah cut a whole paring without having it break and whispered to Martha that in a year or so she'd toss it over her shoulder to find out the initial of the man she would marry. Folks would laugh if she did it this year.

Grandma Sherfey started to sing and everyone joined in. When they sang "Blest Be the Tie That Binds" Martha thought these were the happiest people in Pennsylvania.

Later Mother brought in her birthday cake, beautiful with candles and chocolate icing. Everyone sang "Happy Birthday," and when she blew out the candles it never occurred to her to wish for anything fancy. Instead, she suddenly wished she would grow up and be as happy as Mother.

There's something about Mother—the way she smiles, perhaps. She doesn't need a rose in her bonnet or a pretty dress to make her look beautiful. *Ach,* it's contentment, for all.

Martha poured cup after cup of coffee and served generous helpings of pie as she listened to the talk. What a wonderful thing a snitz party was.

When everyone had gone at last and the kitchen was quiet once more, Martha and Mother cleared away the mess. Father wound the clock, saying casually over his shoulder, "Sam says when they have a drawing of lots for a new minister at Blooming Glen my name will be one of those in the Bible.

"I don't think you liked much having a minister for a grandfather, Martha—how will you like having one for a father?"

Johnny grinned and even Martha had to smile.

"Have you got over feeling bad you can't have a pink dress or a gold ring?" Father added. "Once you said you never would, not so?"

Martha thought a long while before she answered. "Maybe it is seeing how we Plain People work together, almost like we do in our own family, that makes me not mind any more." She looked around the kitchen, her glance resting on Mother's face. "I-yi-yi-yi," she said, "but you were right. Never is a long time!"